W9-CFI-177

The Image of the Stranger Would Not Leave Her Mind.

It was natural that he would stand out. He was the only gringo in the room besides herself. He looked dark and hard and lean, a part of the shadowy night outside. Perhaps he was merely an adventuresome tourist who had drifted into the obscure little Mexican town in search of some action. Perhaps he had wandered into the cantina for the same reason she had: to get a bite to eat and have a bottle of the local beer. Perhaps he was a perfectly innocuous male who, when he realized there was another North American in the cantina, would come over to her table to chat.

Then again, perhaps he was her executioner.

Dear Reader:

Silhouette has always tried to give you exactly what you want. When you asked for increased realism, deeper characterization and greater length, we brought you Silhouette Special Editions. When you asked for increased sensuality, we brought you Silhouette Desire. Now you ask for books with the length and depth of Special Editions, the sensuality of Desire, but with something else besides, something that no one else offers. Now we bring you SILHOUETTE INTIMATE MOMENTS, true romance novels, longer than the usual, with all the depth that length requires. More sensuous than the usual, with characters whose maturity matches that sensuality. Books with the ingredient no one else has tapped: excitement.

There is an electricity between two people in love that makes everything they do magic, larger than life—and this is what we bring you in SILHOUETTE INTIMATE MOMENTS. Look for them wherever you buy books.

These books are for the woman who wants more than she has ever had before. These books are for you. As always, we look forward to your comments and suggestions. You can write to me at the address below:

Karen Solem
Editor-in-Chief
Silhouette Books
P.O. Box 769
New York, N.Y. 10019

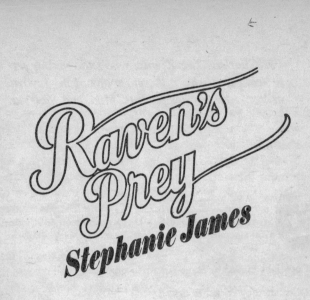

Raven's Prey

Stephanie James

Silhouette Intimate Moments
Published by Silhouette Books New York
America's Publisher of Contemporary Romance

*For Charlene Lee Krentz, who's too young yet
to read, and who is therefore one of my favorite
critics. And for her parents, Mike and Vanessa.*

SILHOUETTE BOOKS, a Division of Simon & Schuster, Inc.
1230 Avenue of the Americas, New York, N.Y. 10020

Copyright © 1983 by Jayne Krentz Incorporated

Distributed by Pocket Books

All rights reserved, including the right to reproduce
this book or portions thereof in any form whatsoever.
For information address Silhouette Books, 1230
Avenue of the Americas, New York, N.Y. 10020

ISBN: 0-671-47529-0

First Silhouette Books printing October, 1983

10 9 8 7 6 5 4 3 2 1

All of the characters in this book are fictitious. Any resem-
blance to actual persons, living or dead, is purely coincidental.

SILHOUETTE and colophon are registered trademarks
of Simon & Schuster, Inc.

SILHOUETTE INTIMATE MOMENTS is a trademark
of Simon & Schuster, Inc.

America's Publisher of Contemporary Romance

Printed in the U.S.A.

Chapter 1

PERHAPS HE WAS MERELY AN ADVENTURESOME TOURIST who had drifted into the obscure little Mexican town in search of some action. Perhaps he had wandered into the cantina for the same reason she had: to get a bite to eat and have a bottle of the local beer. Perhaps he was a perfectly innocuous male who, when he realized there was another North American in the cantina, would come over to her table to chat.

Then again, perhaps he was her executioner.

My God, Honor Knight thought bitterly, I'm really getting paranoid. She forced down another swallow of the robust beer she had been nursing for the last hour and deliberately looked away from the line of men who were standing and leaning with varying degrees of casualness against the bar. That was all she needed now, she chastised herself. She mustn't lose her grip on reality. She must not succumb to genuine paranoia

or life would become intolerable. She really would go out of her mind with fear.

But the image of the stranger as he hooked a booted foot over the bottom rung of the bar would not be banished simply because she chose to look away. It was natural that he would stand out in this crowd, Honor assured herself. He was the only other *gringo* in the room besides herself. Standing at the bar, even lounging against it on one elbow as he was, he topped the Mexican men around him by several inches in most cases.

And while the other men were dressed in the dusty, loose-fitting trousers and shirts of poor, hard-working farmers, the stranger was dark and hard and lean in a pair of black jeans and a black cotton shirt.

His clothes weren't the only things that were dark about him and that made him seem a part of the shadowy night outside. In the brief glance she had allowed herself, Honor had been aware of the deep black shade of his hair. There were subtle highlights of iron-gray in the heavy pelt which indicated the stranger at the bar would soon be staring his fortieth birthday in the face.

Even without the iron in his hair Honor would have been able to guess his age from the unforgiving hardness of his features. Uneasily she allowed her eyes to slide once again over his profile.

He had ordered tequila, not beer, she realized, watching from her sheltered table as he sipped the clear liquor in the small glass he held. How much longer before his roving gaze discovered her against the back wall? She hadn't yet confronted that gaze directly and, based on what she'd seen of the rest of him, Honor didn't particularly want to do so. There

was a ruthless, predatory quality about this man, which disturbed her on several levels. It was there in the hawkish nose, the grimly set mouth and the fiercely etched lines of his face. Somehow he seemed aloof and coldly removed from the scene around him, as if he didn't particularly need human companionship.

Determinedly Honor picked up her fork and took another bite of the corn tamale she had been eating when the newcomer had walked through the door a few minutes earlier. There was nothing to fear, she told herself firmly. After all, she thought on a note of half-hysterical humor, she'd seen plenty of pictures of professional hit men and none of them had ever been wearing jeans and boots! They always seemed to be attired in suits that bulged in the wrong places, and they tended to speak in East Coast accents. Not that she'd heard the stranger when he'd ordered his tequila, but somehow Honor didn't think he would have an eastern accent. More likely a southwestern drawl.

No, she wasn't going to give in to the lure of paranoia. She had to keep a realistic perspective on her present situation or she would become a gibbering idiot! Honor swallowed another sip of the warm beer and resolved to keep her head. It was the only way to survive.

The stranger was probably from Texas or Arizona. Perhaps he had business here in this Mexican village or perhaps he'd merely come south looking for some amusement. One way or another he wasn't a threat to her. He *couldn't* be!

And then she glanced up again and found his night-dark gaze on her.

For an instant everything in the smoky, too-warm

cantina seemed to freeze, including Honor's insides.
She had known instinctively that she didn't want to
meet his eyes directly but instinct hadn't prepared her
for the devastating experience when it finally did
occur.

She had been half expecting a predatory sensuality
in those eyes, Honor realized as her throat went dry.
Casual, masculine lust would have fit with the man
and the scene in which he found himself. After all,
men who wandered into smoke-filled taverns the
world over were usually looking for liquor and a
willing woman. But there was no sign of even the most
superficial desire in his gaze.

If there was no sensuality in his eyes, neither was
there any other emotion she could name. No curiosity, no dislike, no anger, no expectation, no friendli-
ness, no resentment, no humor, *nothing*. Just the
chilling, totally self-contained, nonreflective gleam of
a beast of prey. Honor had never seen such a total
lack of emotion in another human being in her entire
life. In a very real sense it was far more frightening
than if the man had simply pulled a gun and aimed it
at her.

Then he picked up his glass of tequila and started
toward her. In that moment she realized he knew
exactly who she was. The panic threatened to choke
her. It welled up from the pit of her stomach and
literally immobilized her limbs. Desperately she
fought to keep it under control. It was one feeling that
definitely would not aid her now. Unfortunately she
couldn't think of anything that would help her. She
had no choice but to play out her role and pray that
the presence of so many local townspeople there in
the cantina would lend some protection. Did profes-

sional killers have the cold, emotionless eyes of a hawk? It seemed far too likely that they did.

"Honor Knight." Her name was a statement, an identification, not a question, and there *was* a slight southwestern drawl in the low, gravelly intonation of his voice. The dark stranger sat down across from her without bothering with the formality of asking permission. He moved with an easy, smoothly coordinated energy which suggested controlled strength and physical prowess.

When Honor made no response, continuing to sit utterly still staring at him, the man sipped again at his tequila and then asked calmly, "Are you going to make this easy on yourself or are we going to do things the hard way?"

He wasn't armed, Honor told herself frantically. At least not with a gun. It would have bulged somewhere against the fabric of the sleek-fitting jeans and shirt, wouldn't it? Perhaps he used a knife? Or perhaps her imagination had truly run amok. Maybe he wasn't there to kill her. Above all else she must keep her head and not panic.

Knowing that her life depended on staying calm, Honor made herself exchange a level glance with the man across the table. She stifled a shiver as the impenetrable darkness of his gaze met hers. "I'm sorry," she began stiffly, "but you must have mistaken me for someone else. I don't know you and I don't know who it is you think I am but I would appreciate it if you would leave me alone." She tried to make her voice as cold as his eyes.

He watched her silently for a moment and she could almost feel him assessing and cataloging the sum of her features. Good God, how detailed a description had he been given? Could she bluff her way through this? After all, there was nothing all that remarkable about her looks, was there?

She was twenty-nine, but age could be deceptive in a woman hovering between her twenties and her thirties, especially to a man. Her hair was a dark amber brown, but he would probably have been told she was simply a brunette. There were a lot of brunettes in the world, especially in Mexico. And hazel eyes were surely almost as common? Dressed as she was in jeans and a white shirt, her slender figure with its small breasts and gently flaring hips must have appeared similar to the body shapes of countless other women in the world.

"Honor Knight," the man said again and then reached into his shirt pocket and drew out a color photograph. Deliberately he placed it on the table between them, and then he waited. Honor went even colder.

In helpless fascination she stared down at the picture of herself. There, caught by the camera's eye, were all the elements that were so hard to describe verbally, the elements that went together to make each human being distinctive and unique. In her case that meant not just hazel eyes, but wide, intelligent eyes of a complex shade somewhere between green and gold. It meant not just brunette hair but a heavy, amber mane which, although she had recently cut it to shoulder length, still had a characteristic wave even when worn in a clip at the nape of her neck as it was that evening. It meant a mouth that was soft and, in the photo, smiling with feminine warmth. It meant a faintly tip-tilted nose, a proud lift to the chin. It meant no real beauty in the accepted sense but rather an impression of sensitivity, intelligence and a hint of vulnerability.

It meant, Honor realized, disaster. The man could be in no doubt whatsoever that he had found the right woman. Slowly she lifted her eyes from the damning photograph.

"There is also a scar," the stranger went on coolly, "on the left wrist." He reached across the table and caught her hand before she could hide it in her lap. "A mark left over from a botched suicide attempt, I'm told."

She flinched as he captured her hand and exposed the delicate skin on the inside of her wrist. The angry red scar was clearly visible, even in the smoky light.

"A rather badly handled effort," the man observed, his touch remote and dispassionate. "You either didn't want to do a good job or else you must have used a pretty dull knife." He released her hand and Honor shoved her fingers into her lap to hide the trembling in them. "My guess is you probably didn't set out to really take your own life. You probably just used the attempt as a means of getting the kind of attention you seem to need."

"Who are you?" Honor whispered.

"I'm the man who's been sent to bring you home," he said quietly, lifting his tequila glass again. The dark, unfathomable eyes went over her stark expression with a total lack of sympathy or any other emotion. "My name is Judd Raven."

Raven. The name fit him, Honor thought bitterly. A bird of prey. A bird of menace. That explained the eyes, the lack of emotion. The connotations of danger and ill fate that surrounded the word "raven" were not lost on her. In her lap her nails began to eat into the palm of her hand, but her chin stayed proudly lifted.

"Home?" she questioned grimly. There was some cause for hope, she told herself. If he had been sent to fetch her rather than to kill her she still had some chance.

"Your father and brother are damned worried about you," Raven said musingly. "But, then, I suppose you know that, don't you? That's why you're here in the first place."

Her father and brother? "How did they know where I was?"

"They don't. Not precisely. They only knew the general region of Mexico into which you disappeared. They don't speak Spanish themselves so they realized they didn't have much chance of tracing you. That's why they hired me. I've been tracking you for almost a week. You're a foreigner in this country and people remembered the nice *gringa* with the big hazel eyes and the lousy Spanish. It took some legwork but here I am."

"My father and brother," Honor said carefully, "sent you to bring me home?"

He raised his glass in mocking acknowledgment of her apparent slow-wittedness. "Are you disappointed? Would you rather one of them had come with me to look for you? Afraid you won't get as much comfort and attention from me as you would from them?"

"No!"

"What's the matter, Honor? You've achieved almost everything you wanted, haven't you? A lot of time and worry has been spent on you and that's the main thing you were after, wasn't it? This little adventure worked even better than the suicide attempt."

She ignored that, leaning forward to stare at him with wide, searching eyes. "Just tell me the truth. Have you really been sent to bring me home or have you come to kill me?"

He considered the question. "What do you think?"

She blinked and then sat back in her chair, taking in a deep, steadying breath. "I think that if you'd come to kill me I'd probably be dead by now." Which was the truth, she realized. This man wouldn't sit around chatting with his target. He'd get the job over with the efficient cruelty of a hunting bird.

Raven watched the play of emotion across her tightly drawn features. There was a long silence and then he said quietly, "They told me you had a hell of an imagination. That you were borderline paranoid, according to your doctor."

Honor's vulnerable mouth twisted. "I can just imagine what they told you." She stared down at her nearly empty bottle of beer. She had to think, had to find some logical way of dealing with this situation. But it had been almost impossible lately to think logically at all. There had been too much fear and her imagination had been so damn active.

That wonderful, vividly romantic imagination that had always set her apart from her practical, restrained, disapproving family had proven to have a dark side, one which was capable of painting her dreams with nightmarish colors and her daytime thoughts with fear.

Well, there was no point dwelling on that now. At the moment she had to force herself to think very pragmatically indeed. Judd Raven, apparently, was only a hired hand. Or was he merely allowing her to think that so she wouldn't complicate matters by running screaming through the village? "Do you always believe everything you're told, Mr. Raven?"

"No. Sometimes I don't believe anything I'm told."

"That sounds as if you might be suffering from a bit of paranoia yourself!" she challenged wryly.

"I've always felt that a certain degree of paranoia was a useful survival trait," he allowed calmly. "Keeps a man alert."

"Or a woman."

"But in this case," he continued easily, "it doesn't much matter what I believe. I'm just being paid to do a job. I learned a long time ago that it's bad policy to ask too many unnecessary questions."

She bit her lip and watched him broodingly. "What if I said I don't want to return to the States, Mr. Raven?"

"I'd say you don't have a whole hell of a lot of choice."

If he was simply an innocent employee sent to fetch her back, perhaps she could reason with him, Honor told herself resolutely. He might have a policy of not asking questions because he didn't always like the answers. If he cared about answers there might be a chance that he still retained some semblance of a conscience. And if there was a small streak of morality or honor in him somewhere she might be able to appeal to it. It was her only hope.

"Mr. Raven, I am twenty-nine years old. I am not a runaway child. I have the right to go where I please and at the moment I choose to stay here in Mexico. You have no right to try to take me back to the States."

"I think," he said very politely, "that you might as well call me Judd. Something tells me we're going to get to know each other fairly well tonight."

Her sense of shock was plain. There was no point in hiding it. "What's that supposed to mean?" she bit out, a new kind of fear rising beneath the old, familiar variety she had been living with for so long. There was still no sign of masculine desire in those dark eyes but perhaps this man's emotions were so cold that even lust took the form of a chilled passion instead of a heated one. The thought was frightening.

"It means," he said calmly, "that the dirt road I had to use for a landing strip on the other side of the village isn't going to work as a runway at night. I'm not about to risk my neck or my plane trying to take off without being able to see a damn thing. We'll leave in the morning. So I'll be spending the night with you."

Honor shook her head dazedly. "No. I'm not going to leave with you in the morning and I'm not going to spend the night with you. Get out of here, Judd Raven. You don't know what you've gotten yourself involved in. You have no conception of the size of the mess. Get out while you still can. And leave me behind!"

"I don't buy the paranoia act. Your father and brother might believe it and God knows a professional shrink will believe almost anything a patient wants him to believe. But I'm just a hardworking guy who's seen neurotic, spoiled females before. What you probably needed instead of a psychiatrist during your formative years was the application of your father's belt to your backside. But that's his problem. I've only been <u>hired</u> to take you home, not straighten out

your self-centered, childish approach to life." His
mouth kicked upward at the corners in a grimly
amused expression. It was the first sign of any kind of
emotion Honor had seen in him and she didn't like it.
"If I had been hired to straighten you out, I would
have charged a hell of a lot more for the job than I'm
going to get just to fly you home!"

"Just how much are you being paid to kidnap me?"

"Kidnap is a strong word," he noted mildly.

"It's the only word that applies, given the fact that
I'm not going to go with you willingly!" she shot back.

"A couple of thousand plus expenses." He gave her
the answer to her initial question and overlooked the
accusation that had followed.

"A couple of thousand! Is that all?" Was that all a
human life was worth these days? But then he hadn't
been paid to kill her, only to deliver her to the
executioners. "What kind of man are you to do this
sort of thing for a living?" she hissed.

"The kind of man who works for a living." He
appeared totally unperturbed by the taunt. Was there
any way of getting through that wall of indifference?
Could anything reach this man?

Money. If he was doing this for money perhaps that
was the way to get through to him. A few crucial
seconds ticked past as Honor considered the possibility. "A couple of thousand," she repeated carefully.
He nodded in polite agreement, saying nothing. "A
couple of thousand plus expenses," Honor went on,
striving to sound as cool and cynical as he did. "I'll
double that if you'll just go away and leave me here."

He was silent for a long moment and she couldn't
even begin to tell what he was thinking. "They told

me you probably had some money with you," he finally said.

"Everything that was in my bank account," she assured him quickly, daring to let a spark of hope ignite. "All in cash."

"And all belonging to your father," Raven concluded bluntly. "Hell, lady, at your age don't you think it's time you started working for a living instead of sponging off your family? Maybe if you went home and got a job you could learn a little self-discipline, start putting your life in order." He sounded as if the suggested therapy was only of academic interest to him. "Or maybe what you need is marriage to a man who won't let you get away with playing your stupid head games. It's obvious your father has handled you all wrong but the right kind of husband might be able to undo some of the damage and make an adult woman out of you."

"Oh, for God's sake!" she gasped, struggling against the defeating knowledge that she didn't know how to deal with Judd Raven. So much depended on finding the key to this stranger and there was so little time. "Are you interested in ̲ ̲ ̲ ̲ ̲ ̲ ̲ ̲?"

He shook his head briefly ̲ ̲ ̲ ̲ ̲ ̲ so crushed. It was a good try. It's just that I already have a job and accepting your offer would have created a definite conflict of interest, don't you think?"

"I'll triple the offer!" she tried desperately.

"Forget it. Finish your meal and let's go to your place. We've got a long flight ahead of us in the morning and I want to get some sleep." He downed the last of the tequila and sat waiting with the patience of a hunter.

"I seem to have lost my appetite. Listen to me, Judd Raven. If you won't accept my money because you feel it would put you in conflict with my *father's* offer then you must have some sort of business ethics. . . ."

"Business ethics sounds like a fancy term for holding up my end of a deal," he drawled, that faint, frightening amusement lacing his words. "You can call it what you want, but doing the job I've agreed to do is just good business, period. A pilot doesn't need a reputation for unreliability."

"That's what you do for a living? I mean when you're not kidnapping people?" she demanded. More and more it was beginning to look like Judd Raven was merely a tool. If she could somehow render him ineffective she might have a chance.

"I run a small ferrying outfit in New Mexico," he explained with a shrug. "When a businessman in Africa or South America or God-knows-where orders a small private plane from the U.S., he commissions an outfit like mine to fly the aircraft to wherever he is. You don't just pack up a Cessna or a Beechcraft and ship it halfway around the world, you know. It's got to be flown to where it's needed."

"I gather ferrying planes doesn't pay very well, or you wouldn't be obliged to take on outside jobs like kidnapping," Honor snapped impatiently.

"No," he agreed gently, "it doesn't pay all that well. So I sometimes supplement my income with 'outside jobs,' as you put it. Are you finished with that tamale yet?"

Honor looked down at the half-eaten tamale, knowing she was never going to finish it. Her stomach was twisted into one large knot. "Judd," she began evenly, still focusing on the tamale, "will you at least listen to my side of the story?"

He reached across the table and closed iron fingers around her wrist. "You can tell me your side of the story on the way back to Arizona. Come on, Honor, it's getting late. Let's go."

"No, please!"

But he was already on his feet, drawing her up beside him. Throwing a handful of pesos down on the table, Judd Raven turned and led Honor out of the smoky cantina and into the balmy Mexican night. Instinctively Honor tried to fight the steady, inexorable grasp on her wrist but he simply ignored her efforts as he started down the dusty street. After a moment it was obvious he knew where she lived, and Honor felt a new rush of despair. He must have asked about her before locating her in the cantina.

"Won't you at least listen to me?" she pleaded as he led her down the nearly silent street to the small cottage she had rented from the woman who owned the cantina. Aside from the crowd in the tavern there was very little sign of life at this hour. This was a farming community and most people were in bed early. The lack of electricity in many of the homes did not encourage late hours, either.

"In the morning." Judd sighed. "I really don't feel like listening to fairy tales tonight. I've had a long, hard day."

Something about the way he said that told Honor there was no hope of ever getting him to listen to her side of the matter. As far as Judd Raven was concerned he had accepted a job and would see it through to the end. It undoubtedly suited him to know as little as possible about the details of a situation like this,

Honor realized bitterly. He simply wanted to collect his pay and go on to the next job.

If there was no hope of talking her way out of the situation then she really had no alternative but to use the gun. The thought of the deadly little weapon lying in the drawer beside her bed brought little comfort. In her heart of hearts she had prayed she would never have to use it. What was it going to be like, aiming that thing at another human being? Especially a human being who was only a tool, not the real source of danger? Would she really be able to pull the trigger if Judd Raven challenged her? He didn't seem like the kind of man who would bluff very easily.

But she had no choice. She had only herself to rely on. If Honor didn't defend herself, no one would. Lifting her chin, she straightened her shoulders and began to deliberately summon the kind of resolve it would take to remove the wicked little gun from the bedside drawer.

Her cottage was one of the more comfortable structures in town. It was blessed with a naked light bulb which dangled precariously from the ceiling, a very old bathroom and a small electric burner. Other than the bathroom there was only one room, which served as both living room and bedroom. The few pieces of furniture were threadbare and dilapidated.

"You've been living here for four weeks?" Judd asked as he stepped through the door and scanned the stark interior. "I should think you'd be more than ready to go home by now!"

"Nobody's asking you to spend the night here," she muttered tightly, her eyes straying quickly to the nightstand beside the single bed. "Perhaps you'd rather sleep in your plane?" she added icily.

"No, thanks. I've slept in worse places than this. I just have a hard time imagining you being content here. It's hardly Acapulco!"

"But, then, you don't really know me, do you?" she shot back, freeing her wrist to walk restlessly across the small room. She stood staring out the uncurtained window, her back toward the tall, dark man behind her. "You don't know me at all."

There was a strange silence and then Judd said quietly, "You forget I've not only been told a great deal about you but I've been looking at that damned photograph your father gave me for a solid week."

She swung around angrily. "The photograph! What the hell can you learn from a picture?"

"Not much, apparently," he retorted unconcernedly. "Based on that photo I would have said you were a different sort of person than your father and brother described. In fact, when I first saw you in that cantina tonight I would have said you were . . . Never mind. You're just not quite what I had imagined. Which only goes to show," he went on carelessly, examining the bed, "how deceptive appearances can be."

"Somehow I get the impression your appearance isn't deceptive in the least," Honor gritted. "You look exactly like you seem to be. A cold, hard, inhuman man who's only interested in collecting his pay for this dirty little job."

"Now that we understand each other," he said smoothly, "let's get ready for bed, shall we? You don't have to look at me like that, you know. I'll be sleeping on the floor. That lumpy mattress doesn't look much more comfortable than these boards, anyway. You're welcome to it."

Honor stood still beside the window, watching as

Judd methodically confiscated a couple of the worn blankets and spread them out on the floor. When he'd finished he glanced up, examining her tense face. "I have to get a couple of things out of the plane. You'd better come with me." He turned abruptly toward the door and opened it. When she made no move to follow he glanced back and said laconically, "I know there's nowhere you can run in this village. I'm aware of the fact that you left your car back in the States and that you traveled through Mexico on buses. You probably can't get into too much trouble in the ten minutes it's going to take me to get my things from the plane, but just the same I'll feel more comfortable if you're with me. I wouldn't want to return to find you've made another halfhearted attempt on your wrists."

Honor went white. "Damn you!" she whispered savagely.

"Come here, Honor," he ordered quietly. "Don't make me drag you through the streets to the plane and back."

It was a small thing, this business of ordering her to cross the room and accompany him, but Honor sensed immediately that he was doing it deliberately. Judd was establishing the rules, making it clear that he was in charge. He probably thought that if he took a firm enough position she would simply give up and stop fighting him. As far as he was concerned she was a spoiled brat who happened to be nearly thirty. Spoiled brats were traditionally best handled by a dose of discipline.

Didn't he realize that when you were fighting for your life you didn't play by anyone else's rules?

Still, this was not the time to go into battle.

Common sense dictated that she give an appearance, at least, of resigning herself to her lot. Honor's sensitive mouth tightened ominously but she silently crossed the room.

"That's better," Judd approved, opening the door. "Behave yourself and we'll get along just fine."

Perhaps, Honor decided objectively, it wouldn't be so difficult using the gun on him later! The man had it coming.

The Cessna 185/Skywagon was perched in the desert on the side of the dirt road into town. In the moonlight Honor could see the high wings and the old-fashioned tailwheel. It was painted a light color, difficult to discern in the shadows. She hated it on sight. Up until now there had been a pleasant feeling of isolation and remoteness about the small Mexican village. There were few cars in town and only a weekly bus. The plane removed that sensation of being out of touch with civilization. Once on board the Cessna she would be lost.

Judd opened the cabin door on the pilot's side and reached into the cockpit to remove a small, weatherbeaten overnight bag. Honor watched in silence as he checked the inside of the cabin and then she waited a few more minutes while he verified that the wheels were firmly chocked. She watched his hand linger for another few seconds on the tail as he gave a last, assessing glance at the preparations he had made, and suddenly Honor realized that he must have already checked out the plane for the night. The current attention was probably wholly unnecessary. But there was something in the way he touched the metal and eyed the wheels that annoyed her in a way she couldn't quite explain.

"Is that plane the only thing you care about? You act as if you're tucking it in for the night!" she muttered disgustedly.

"The plane and I have an understanding," he told her dryly. "I take care of it and it takes care of me. As a companion it has definite virtues. No tantrums, no back talk, no arguments."

"How dull for you!" Honor spun around on her heel, plunged her hands disconsolately into the back pockets of her jeans and started back along the road into town.

"I suppose it would seem a little dull to you," Judd allowed quietly. He paced beside her with that long, flowing stride of his, which was coming to remind her of a lazily circling bird of prey. "After all, you apparently thrive on causing scenes and creating chaos. I prefer a quieter sort of life."

"Ferrying planes around the globe is a quiet life?" she scoffed, not looking at him.

"Do you have any idea what it's like to be alone in the cabin of a small aircraft for up to eighteen hours straight? No one to talk to, nothing to keep you going except coffee and sandwiches? It's quiet, all right! The world feels empty."

"I didn't think small private planes carried enough fuel for that long a trip," Honor muttered, telling herself she really didn't want to start a conversation with him. Now that she had decided to use the gun she realized she didn't want to talk to him at all. Talking brought the danger of communication, and communication meant a risk of understanding. She didn't want to understand or communicate with a man she might have to shoot later.

"The planes are outfitted with special long-distance tanks for the ferrying trips."

"Oh."

"It has its compensations, you know," he went on softly. "My business, I mean."

"It sounds pretty damn frightening to me! I can't imagine being alone in a small airplane out over the middle of the Atlantic. If things went wrong . . ." She shuddered, an image of lonely terror streaking through her mind.

"Yes." He was silent for a moment. "But there are other times. Times when the sun is coming up and you feel like you're the only person alive in the world to see it. Or when you're flying over a deserted stretch of jungle and you realize what the world must have been like when it was younger."

She risked a quick look at him, her gaze sliding off his hard profile as soon as it touched. "You're a real loner, aren't you?"

"Most of the people in my line of work are," he said dismissingly. "I guess that's why we get into the business in the first place."

"It must be strange feeling closer to an airplane than to other human beings!" Honor didn't attempt to hide the scorn in her voice.

"It must be strange to need the attention of other human beings so badly that you resort to things like fake suicide attempts and running off to deserted Mexican villages." There was no scorn in his words, only a kind of aloof disapproval.

Honor bit back the angry, useless protest that rose to her lips and lapsed into sullen silence for the rest of the walk into town.

Judd bedded down by the door, blocking the only means of escape from the one-room shack. Honor watched him resentfully as he put out the single light and slid between the thin blankets. He didn't bother to undress and neither did she. As far as she could tell he went to sleep at once, his head pillowed on a rolled-up towel.

Lying tensely on the cot that had served as her bed for the past month Honor felt each minute that passed as if it were an eternity. For her own protection she had to make certain Judd Raven was asleep before she reached for the gun in the drawer beside her. With that swift, gliding way he moved he could be upon her before she could get her hand into the drawer if he realized her intentions in time.

She waited fifteen minutes and then she waited another ten. During that time Raven never moved. How could he sleep so easily on that hard board floor?

At last, when the moonlight outside had shifted a few degrees on the windowsill, Honor told herself that the time had come. It was now or never. She had to get hold of the gun and then wake her captor, letting him know he was no longer the one in charge.

Moving with a slowness that was almost painful, Honor slid her arm out from under the old sheet and groped blindly for the drawer pull. Her heart pounded with the tension of the moment and she wondered briefly how Judd could keep from being awakened by it. It took an effort of will to control her breathing. Thank God she had taken the time to practice with the weapon after she'd bought it off that sleazy street vendor just across the border into Mexico. But she'd never used it on any living thing, Honor reminded herself. It wasn't going to be easy this first time.

And then her fingers closed on the old wooden knob of the drawer. Holding her breath tightly in her throat, Honor tugged cautiously. The slight scrape of the wood didn't cause any response from Judd. He really was sound asleep.

With a swallowed sigh Honor touched the cold metal of the gun. It came into her hand like an alien thing, chilled and deadly. For an instant she almost lost her nerve. *She had never used it on a living thing. Not even a field mouse!*

Gripping the weapon tightly Honor sat up slowly in bed. She used both hands to aim while she slid quietly out of bed. When she was on her feet she tried to find her voice and nearly failed.

"J-Judd," she managed, aware of the fact that she was trembling from head to foot. "Judd, wake up. We're going to talk."

He didn't stir and for an instant she thought she had failed to waken him. Honor was moistening her lips, about to try again when his voice came floating across the room in a low, sleepy growl.

"Go back to sleep, Honor. I've got the bullets in my pocket."

Honor stilled in sudden shock, knowing somehow, even before she tried to fire the gun, that she'd been outmaneuvered.

"No, damn you! *No!*" She raised the weapon to a level well above his reclining form and pulled the trigger. There was only a dry click to tell her there was no bullet in the chamber. "Damn you to hell, Judd Raven!" Fury broke free within her, overshadowing all the other emotions she had been experiencing that evening.

Fury and hatred for the man who had so casually

foiled her one hope of escape made her draw back her arm and hurl the useless weapon at him with a savagery that surprised even herself.

She heard him swear softly as the small weapon struck his leg. Then in a frustrated rage she followed the gun, throwing herself across the room and down onto his recumbent form.

"Damn you! Damn you! Damn you!" With the ferocity of a cornered cat Honor lashed out at her captor, her flailing fingers going for his eyes.

Chapter 2

THE BATTLE WAS OVER ALMOST BEFORE IT HAD BEGUN, and if she'd been thinking coherently in those first few seconds of anger and panic, Honor would have realized there could be only one ending.

But logical thought was not what was driving her as she launched herself at Judd Raven. And because she was beyond realizing the hopelessness of the attack, she was able to carry it further than it normally would have gone.

Raven didn't fight back, which was the one thing that would have ended it quickly. Given his superior size and strength he could have knocked her sprawling with a couple of cuffs. Instead he seemed to absorb the brunt of her fury, catching her wrists so that she couldn't get at his eyes, but otherwise not seeking to retaliate.

"Calm down, you little hellcat," he grunted as she

tried to knee him. He barely managed to deflect the blow, shifting his body so that she was trapped beneath him. "Honor, settle down! This isn't going to do any good and you know it!"

But she refused to listen to the advice, surging and struggling and scrabbling upward against his steadily increasing weight. When one of her legs came free momentarily she kicked at him and he grunted in pain. One of her hands got near his cheek and she raked furiously with her nails, gouging deep enough to draw blood.

"Honor! Stop it! Don't make me hurt you!" His grip on her wrists tightened and he threw his leg heavily over her twisting lower body. "Stop it!"

"Let me go, you damned mercenary! Let me go or so help me I won't stop trying to kill you all the way back to Arizona!" she cried, gasping for breath even as she felt her strength draining rapidly.

"You're out of your head!"

"I know! I'm crazy, remember? I'm supposed to be under the care of a psychiatrist at all times!" Viciously she snapped her teeth, trying to take a chunk out of his forearm. She only got a mouthful of black cotton fabric for her efforts.

"Honor, if you don't stop fighting me I'm going to have to hurt you!" he gritted. He caught both of her wrists in one of his hands, stretching her arms over her head and pinning them to the floor.

"Go ahead," she taunted violently, her small breasts heaving as she tried to draw air into her lungs. "Go ahead and hurt me! Show me what a tough man you really are! But whatever you do, it had better be pretty violent because unless you cripple me I'm going to keep trying to escape!"

She was almost totally helpless now, pinned beneath his weight, her hands useless. Her head twisted on the floor, amber hair fanning out against the boards, and in the shadows her hazel eyes flashed fire.

"Honor, just give up, will you? Pack it in, lady, you haven't got a chance!"

"I know," she rasped. "I've also got nothing left to lose."

"For God's sake, woman, be sensible! All I'm trying to do is take you home! I can't figure you out, you know that? You seem too damned smart, too much like a real woman to resort to this kind of thing. Why the hell do you insist on acting like a child?"

She heard the genuine lack of comprehension in his voice and wanted to laugh hysterically. It was impossible to move now. Her whole body was completely trapped by his superior strength. All she could do was lie there looking up at him in the darkness with all the impotent fury of a beaten but unbowed woman in her eyes.

"Are you going to behave?" he demanded, eyes narrowed as he studied her defiant face.

"Sure," she spat.

He sighed. "Honor, if you're not going to be reasonable—"

"Most people become unreasonable when their lives are at stake!"

"Don't give me that paranoia routine!" he ordered. "I told you earlier this evening, I don't buy it!"

"Too bad! I'm going to fight you every step of the way, Judd Raven. As I said earlier, I haven't got anything left to lose!"

"Do you want to spend the whole trip tied to the seat of my plane?" he snarled warningly.

"Is that the only way you know to handle a twenty-nine-year-old spoiled brat?" she taunted furiously.

Something new flickered in the depths of his dark eyes and then it was gone. "No," he told her in a deadly voice, "there are other ways of dealing with a woman."

"Are you threatening to rape me or beat me?" Her only weapon now was her tongue and Honor used it recklessly. She felt driven to taunt and goad him until she could get some kind of human response out of him. If she could find a crack in the seemingly impenetrable wall that surrounded him, perhaps she would have a chance of reaching him.

Or perhaps she would find there was simply nothing beneath that barrier except more of the same unnaturally cold, hard maleness that seemed to assault her senses.

"Which would you prefer?" he retorted brutally. "Would you rather be raped or beaten into submission? Is this part of the syndrome, Honor? Has your infantile brain somehow concluded that violence is a form of attention, too?"

"There's no real choice, is there?" she hissed scornfully. "You'll have to beat me into submission because you're incapable of raping me!"

"Damn it to hell, woman!"

"It's true, isn't it? Even rape takes some kind of emotion. Hatred, sadism, a sick kind of passion, *something!* You don't have any emotions that run that deep, do you? Not even old-fashioned, garden-variety lust!"

Suddenly the dark eyes of the hunting bird gleamed dangerously in the moonlight. Honor felt Judd go very still above her, his body tight with a new kind of tension. She held her breath, knowing she had pushed him much too far and knowing, too, that she'd had no choice.

"Do you know what you're doing?" he whispered harshly.

Honor felt as if she were caught up in the talons of a bird of prey but her eyes never left his. "So it's going to be the beating, is it? I thought so. When was the last time you went to bed with a woman, Judd Raven? I'll bet it's been years! Tell me, do you make love to that damned plane—"

The words were cut off in her throat as his head swooped down toward hers. She had only time enough to read the glittering fury in his eyes, time enough to realize that at least she had sparked some kind of emotion in him and then his mouth was on hers in savage conquest.

The impact of the brutal kiss washed through her body like a crashing wave. It was far more than Honor had bargained for, even in her desperation to goad Judd into some kind of response. She lay passively beneath the assault, unable even to drag her mouth free of his.

She had never known anything like it before in her whole life. There was no finesse, no pretense at romance, no hint of tenderness. The kiss could not even be described as passionate. It was overwhelming and devastating, a primitive attempt by a man to dominate a woman in the most fundamental sense. Judd's mouth moved on hers with feral intent, forcing apart her lips. When she instinctively tried to close her teeth against the invasion of his tongue, he used his thumb and forefinger on her jaw to pry open her mouth. Then he was inside, swamping her senses, exploring and conquering every corner.

The faint moan of protest and newfound fear which emanated from deep in her throat went unheeded. Judd's free hand slid roughly down her throat to find her breast and closed over the gentle curve of it. She trembled violently beneath the onslaught, terrified at what she had unleashed.

His legs slid between hers, pushing her thighs apart in a gesture that left her feeling ravished even though she was still dressed. Crushed as she was against the unyielding wooden floor, Honor began to panic. The tremors coursing through her were uncontrollable. Tears seeped into her eyes and she closed them tightly.

It was the ripple of small, violent shivers in her body that finally got through to Judd. He sensed the fear as if it were a tangible presence emanating from her and her total vulnerability finally registered in his raging mind.

What was she doing to him? What in God's name had he allowed her to do to him? And what the hell was the matter with him that he had gone off the deep end like this?

The fury surging through him didn't disintegrate, but his normal iron control finally began to reassert itself. He fought back the waves of enraged desire that were still pouring through his body, breathing heavily with the effort. One hand closed into a tight, hard fist of frustration and anger. He wrenched his mouth from hers and stared down at the lips he had bruised with his own.

Such a soft mouth. It had been one of the first

things he had noticed about her. That gentle mouth and those huge hazel eyes. Every time he had looked at that damned photo he had wondered how that mouth and those eyes could belong to the self-centered, immature, spoiled brat of a woman he had been sent to find. He hadn't wanted to think of her as genuinely crazy for some reason, although that explanation was probably the simplest one. So he had studied the intelligent eyes with their hint of mischief and humor and decided that the woman he was after was merely overindulged by a doting family. It had crossed his mind more than once that the right man might be able to straighten her out.

Not that he was that man, Judd had assured himself as he tramped through the dusty streets of one village after another. He was merely making an observation.

Now here he was almost raping her. And it was all her fault. She was more than spoiled and overindulged. She was dangerous.

"Damn it, lady, what kind of game are you playing?" he ground out. "You're even sicker than your family thinks you are if this is the way you get your kicks!"

Her eyes slitted open and he saw the trace of tears in their gold-and-green depths as she watched him with the expression of a trapped animal. But even though he could see the remains of genuine fear in her eyes her tongue continued to cut at him like a knife.

"If I really was trying to get my thrills this way it's obvious I'm in for a disappointment, isn't it?"

He swore softly, violently. "Why are you trying to goad me into rape, you stupid woman? What is it with you?"

"Maybe I just wanted to see if there was some trace

of an identifiable human emotion in you," she mocked scathingly. "You're like a robot, Judd Raven. I've been trying to talk to you all evening, argue with you, plead with you and all I got was the feeling I'm dealing with a damned robot!"

"So you decided to see if you could provoke me, is that it? After trying to shoot me, first, that is!"

"I didn't shoot you! I never got the chance, remember? You stole the bullets from my gun. When did you do that, Judd? Before you came looking for me in the cantina?" she blazed furiously.

"I thought it might be wise to search this place before going to look for you. And I was right, wasn't I? Where did you get that piece of garbage you call a gun? Tijuana? Talk about a cheap 'Saturday night special'!"

"It must have been enough to scare you or you wouldn't have bothered disarming me!"

"It made me a little nervous, all right. Any kind of weapon in the hands of an unpredictable female like yourself is grounds for making a man nervous." He released her with a short, disgusted oath, sitting up beside her. "But it turns out you've got some hidden weapons, doesn't it?"

"I was desperate. I *am* desperate." She edged away from him warily, sitting up and curling her legs under herself as she watched him. "I'll do anything I can to make you listen to me."

"That's obvious. Including getting yourself raped. You think that would really have done any good? Did you think I'd be so weakened afterward that you'd be able to make your escape?" he scoffed, annoyed because it was possible she was right. Taking this hellion would probably exhaust any man. To be on the safe side one would have to be certain that she knew who was in charge first. She would use any scrap of power she thought she had.

"I wasn't trying to get myself raped!" she bit out. "It's just that everything seemed so hopeless after I realized the gun was empty. . . ." Her voice trailed off despairingly and she looked away from him.

In the moonlight he examined her profile and remembered how she had looked a few minutes earlier holding the gun on him. "The gun wouldn't have worked, Honor," he finally said with a gentleness that surprised him. "Even if it had been loaded."

Her head swung around. "What do you mean?"

He moved one hand in a small gesture of dismissal. "When you tried a shot to see whether or not I was telling the truth about the bullets, you didn't even aim the gun at me. If there had been a bullet, it would have gone through the door about three feet over my head. You should have aimed it at me. It might have been the only chance you got. Never threaten a man with a gun unless you're prepared to use it."

"I was prepared to use it!"

He shook his head. "No, you'd nerved yourself up to threaten me with it but not to use it on me. Even if I hadn't gotten the bullets out of it earlier, I could have taken the gun away from you a few minutes ago."

She glared at him. "You're wrong, you know. I'm quite desperate. Why can't I make you see that?"

"I realize you're desperate," he soothed, "but there's no need to be and you know it. I'm only going to take you home, Honor. What's so horrible about that?"

"The people you're taking me back to will probably kill me," she declared flatly. "They might kill you, too, come to think of it. They'll be wondering how much I've told you during the time we're together."

"Honor," he began carefully, thinking of the worried, deeply concerned father waiting back in Arizona, "listen to me—"

"No," she interrupted, "you listen to me. You're nothing but a damned mercenary. You're doing this for the money, aren't you?"

Why did the accusation offend him? Judd wondered. His mouth tightened. "It's a job."

"All right, it's a job and it pays a couple of thousand plus expenses, right? I'll double that if you'll just—"

"I've told you, I'm going to do the job I was hired to do!" he snapped. Didn't the woman ever give up?

"I'm not asking you to renege on your lousy contract! I'm offering to buy a couple of days of your time! How about it, Judd. Two thousand dollars for two days."

Anger flashed in him. "Now what are you trying to do?"

She leaned forward intently, putting a hand on his arm. He felt the contact of her fingers and something in him reacted to it. Grimly he refused to give any indication of that reaction, forcing himself to sit like stone beneath her touch.

"Two days, Judd. I want to buy two lousy days. Is that so much to ask? The people who sent you after me will never know, will they? They can't have any way of knowing you've even found me yet. How long did you tell them it might take?"

His eyes narrowed. "I told them to give me a couple

of weeks, maybe a month." Now why the devil had he told her that much?

"You can double your take on this job by simply staying here in this village with me for a couple of days," she explained. "I'll give you the money up front. Tonight. All I want is your word that during the next two days you'll give me a chance to tell you my side of this story. Think of it. Two thousand dollars for two days of humoring me. Surely you can't afford to ignore that kind of offer?"

"What is it with you, lady? You've tried just about everything tonight. Bribery, a gun and sex. Just to buy a couple of days' worth of time here in this flea-bitten shack?"

"I didn't try sex!" Honor didn't know why she felt obliged to clarify that point. The desperate wish to provoke some sort of identifiable male reaction in him hadn't been a thought-out plan. It had been an instinctive, intuitive action which had nearly backfired. "And you needn't worry that I'll try that tactic during the next two days, either. I only want a chance to tell my side of this mess."

He looked down at the hand on his arm and Honor immediately withdrew it, folding it tensely into a small fist which she rested against her thigh. When Judd's eyes met hers again in the shadowy light she could see a trace of the savage glitter she'd elicited a few minutes earlier when she'd taunted him.

"You did try sex," Judd growled softly. "And your efforts nearly got you raped. That's all you would have achieved, Honor, believe me. Taking you physically would not have made me more vulnerable to your arguments and schemes. I want that very clear between us. I want you to understand that seducing me isn't going to buy you a damn thing except a night in bed with me. It's certainly not going to convince me not to take you back to Arizona."

She flinched under the harsh impact of his words even as she registered the fact that his tone was at last carrying some nuance of emotion. He was still angry at her for causing him to nearly lose his self-control, she realized vaguely. There wasn't time now to sort out what that might mean, but she stored it away for future reference.

"I'm not talking about sex. I'm talking about money. I understand that money probably holds a lot more interest for you under the circumstances," she retorted.

Once more a measure of fury, quickly checked, flashed into those raven-dark eyes, but when he spoke again Judd had himself firmly under control. "I've told you that you can tell me your story on the trip back to Arizona in the morning. It can't be that long a tale!"

"I want more time than the few hours it will take to fly me back to the States!"

"Time to convince me."

"Yes, damn it! Believe it or not, I get the feeling that if I can just drum the truth into your thick skull I might have a chance of surviving this disaster. I'm banking on the fact that you wouldn't willingly turn me over to people who want to kill me. Not if you know the truth."

"What gives you so much faith in my integrity?" he mocked.

"Maybe it's not a case of having any faith in your integrity," she shot back heatedly. "Maybe it's just a feeling that you've got sense enough to look out for yourself. And getting involved in murder might cause you more than a couple of thousand dollars' worth of trouble. If I can make you see that, I might be able to get you to leave me here in Mexico. You'll be able to go home to your precious airplane-ferrying business with the two thousand you left it to collect and without having gotten yourself mixed up with murder."

"You throw a big word like murder around pretty freely, Honor. I wonder if you have any idea of what you're saying?"

"Believe me, I know what I'm talking about!" she breathed.

"God, maybe your shrink is right. Maybe you really are borderline paranoid. Maybe you're already over the border," he muttered.

"But you don't believe that, do you?" Honor challenged, suddenly aware that she had found a wedge. "You don't think I'm really crazy. You think I'm just spoiled and difficult and childish. But would even a spoiled brat carry a tantrum this far? You think I've enjoyed living in this shack for the past few weeks? You think I like not being able to have a conversation with anyone in my own language? You think I like having to boil every drop of water I drink because I'm afraid I'll get sick? You think it's been pleasant doing without a telephone or a refrigerator or a car? For God's sake, Judd. Spoiled brats don't like to go too long without their creature comforts, do they? I would have headed for Acapulco or one of the other tourist centers if I'd just been trying to upset my family. Why would I make myself suffer in the process?"

"You tried suicide once," he pointed out inexorably. "Someone who did that might have some strange notions of how to make others suffer. Maybe living like this"—he waved a hand vaguely around the shack—"is your idea of punishing your father in some way."

Honor closed her eyes in hopeless frustration. "There's no reasoning with you, is there?" she finally asked in a dead voice.

Silence greeted the question and when she opened her eyes again it was to find him watching her with a long, brooding stare. "If," Judd began cautiously, "I agreed to give you two days, would you be willing to promise me that you won't give me any trouble when the time comes to take you home?"

Honor swallowed, not quite believing her ears. "Do you mean that? You'll grant me the time?"

"I might." Why the hell was he even considering the damn bargain? He should just tie her up hand and foot, throw her into the plane and leave at dawn tomorrow morning. But once he had delivered her to her family he would probably never see her again. And after having searched for her for nearly a week, Judd was beginning to realize that he wanted a little time with this woman. Time to determine whether or not there was anything real beneath the soft mouth and the big eyes. Two days wasn't going to matter one way or the other, he told himself, knowing even as he did so that he was rationalizing the situation. "But in return I'd want your personal guarantee that you'll give me no trouble when it comes time to leave."

"You have it," she vowed rashly, her relief shimmering in her eyes. Once again she impulsively put out a hand and touched his arm. "I swear you have it.

Just give me a couple of days to explain this whole mess to you. Then, if you don't believe me—"

"You'll start in all over again, won't you?" he groaned. "I'm a fool to let myself get talked into this."

"The worst thing that can happen to you is that you'll make an extra two thousand dollars!" she stormed.

Damn it, why did she have to keep harping on the money? "No that's not the worst thing that can happen to me," he shot back bluntly. "The worst thing is that I'll give you the impression that I'm a fool of a man who can be manipulated."

"But I don't think that!" she protested, snatching her hand away again. He felt the loss of the warmth of her fingers and wondered at it. He liked having her touch him spontaneously, Judd acknowledged silently.

"Yes, you do. At this point in time you do." He sighed. "Just don't go overboard with the idea, though, because you'll only be deluding yourself. Go back to bed, Honor. You can start talking in the morning. I really don't think I'm up to hearing the wild tale tonight."

"But it won't take me long to give you a rough outline of what really happened and then you can ask questions—" she began earnestly.

"Honor, so far you've threatened me with a gun, attacked me physically—yes you did," he injected when she started to protest. He touched the side of his face meaningfully. "Something tells me I'll be wearing a few scars tomorrow. And you nearly provoked me into taking you by force. In all honesty you'll have to admit I've suffered enough tonight. Let the explanations ride until tomorrow, okay? I'm tired, even if you aren't."

She didn't want to retreat to her cot, he realized. She wanted to sit there on the floor and give him the whole crazy tale she'd concocted. She was a determined little thing, he had to hand it to her.

"Bed, Honor," he repeated levelly.

"Oh, all right," she said, scrambling to her feet. "But you will listen in the morning, won't you? With an open mind? You'll give me a chance to explain?"

"I'll listen. I'm making no promises beyond that." He refused to let himself offer any further comfort and as she turned back to the cot he was aware of her mixed reaction. She was depressed because she hadn't completely gained the upper hand and relieved because at least she'd accomplished something with her fierce attack. What kind of female was he dealing with? Judd asked himself for the thousandth time.

He lay back down on the hard floor, adjusting the makeshift pillow and the tattered blanket. Across the small expanse of space separating them he watched her climb back into bed and pull the covers up around her chin.

The thought that had been hovering at the back of his mind ever since he'd walked into the cantina finally came forward: *She was real.*

My God, was she real, he repeated, touching the small wound on his cheek with a grimace. He had the marks to prove it now.

But for the past few days he had felt as if he were chasing down a fantasy. It had made him uneasy at first, telling everyone he met that she was his runaway wife, but gradually the fiction had seemed to cross the bounds of reality in his own mind. Every time he glanced at the photo he had wondered what it would be like to have a real claim on her, to know that when he found her he could keep her.

Loneliness had never been a problem before, Judd thought fleetingly. He'd been on his own for so long that he had a hard time imagining any other sort of life. He preferred being alone. It was natural for him now. A habit. People who lived with each other had skills he couldn't even comprehend. They laughed together and they talked together. Flying airplanes seemed a whole lot easier and a hell of a lot less demanding. Since the day he'd gotten his license, airplanes had seemed a good substitute for the unreliable friendship of humans, especially women.

No, being alone had become a way of life and he had been stoically satisfied with his path. Until this past week when he had found himself tracking down a woman he was claiming as his wife. What would it have been like, he'd wondered, if she really had been his mate? What would it be like to have a woman who was his and his alone? Since the day he'd been left to the casual care of a series of foster homes he'd had no one he could really claim as his own. As a man he had known women but he'd never had the feeling that any of them truly belonged to him. And none had seemed anxious to claim him permanently, either.

But a strange new sensation of possessiveness had grown within him as he'd traced Honor through Mexico. It filled him with a restlessness that he didn't understand.

It was only then, as silence descended and a semblance of superficial peace settled on the room, that

Judd allowed himself to think about what he had felt when he'd lain on top of Honor Knight and trapped her soft, twisting body with his own.

It would have taken very little to push him completely over the edge during those few minutes. His body hadn't completely quieted down even yet. It was easy to imagine what it would have been like to tear off her shirt and find the curves of her breasts. He could almost feel the budding nipples beneath his palms. And if he'd gone that far he wouldn't have been able to stop. Judd drew a long breath, knowing he could easily have unsnapped her jeans and stripped them from her hips, leaving her open and vulnerable. She might have fought like a wildcat but she was no match for his masculine strength. He could have slid between her legs and buried himself in her warmth, taking her completely.

And it would have been good. So good. Damn it to hell. His body was hardening again just at the imagery. Maybe he should have taken her, Judd told himself violently. She had certainly been asking for it the way she had first attacked and then taunted him.

Maybe he should have taken her and taught her that she couldn't get away with treating him first as if he were some kind of mercenary bounty hunter and then as if he were impotent. Christ! The woman sure knew how to get at a man! No wonder her father and brother were in such a turmoil over her. She must have been running them ragged for years.

Honor Knight needed someone to take her in hand, Judd decided not for the first time that week. She needed a man who could control her, one whom she couldn't manipulate. Once that crazy quirk in her personality was straightened out, the one that made her grab for unnatural attention and try to manipulate every man in her orbit, she might be one hell of a woman. She didn't lack guts and she didn't give up easily. Furthermore, there was a sensuality about her which intrigued him far more than he wanted to admit.

What would have happened if he had, indeed, taken her? Judd finally dozed off into a light sleep with that question still burning in his mind and in his loins.

Chapter 3

THE FAMILIAR KNOCK OF THE NEIGHBORHOOD BOY WHO brought her fresh eggs three times a week brought Honor out of her restless sleep the next morning. As she struggled awake she automatically glanced across the room. The bedding Judd had been using during the night was neatly folded and stashed on the crate that served as an end table. From the tiny bathroom she could hear the sound of running water. He must be shaving, Honor decided, pulling herself out of bed and padding barefoot across the floor to open the door.

"Buenos días, Paco.¿Qué tal?" Judd might have been right about her Spanish being lousy but it had been improving daily in this land of strangers who spoke no English.

The small, black-haired boy on the front step grinned up at her and shyly handed her the carton of eggs. "I am fine," he answered formally in Spanish, remembering to slow down so that she could understand him. "I've brought your eggs."

"Wonderful. I'll go and get the money." Honor didn't kid herself. This was a poor village and her willingness to pay well for good food and vegetables was much appreciated locally. Solemnly she counted out the proper amount for the eggs, the coins disappearing into the child's grubby little hand.

"My mother wants to know if you'll be needing more eggs now that your man has found you?" Paco asked gravely, peering unabashedly around the corner to see if he could catch sight of the stranger who had taken the *gringa* out of the cantina last night.

"Tell your mother that I'll let her know," Honor told him dryly. In a small town like this the arrival of Judd Raven was hardly likely to go unnoticed.

"Do you think your man will give me a ride in his airplane?" Paco asked hurriedly.

Honor didn't catch every word but she got the gist of the question. "You'll have to ask him," she said smiling, and in the back of her mind a glimmering of an idea began to take shape. The airplane was the means by which Judd Raven eventually planned to get her out of the country. He would never let her near the Cessna unescorted but he was going to have a hard time keeping all the curious village children from hanging around the exotic machine. If worse came to worst and Raven refused to pay any heed to her explanation, those children might offer her a possible way of sabotaging that damned plane.

"Ask me what?" Judd's voice cut across her thoughts as he emerged from the bathroom behind her, wiping his neck with a small towel he'd found.

The dark shadow of his beard, which had been evident last night, was gone temporarily, but in the bright morning light he reminded her just as much of a black-winged bird of prey as he had the night before.

Honor took in the brilliant midnight eyes, the emotionless expression on his bronzed face and the hard lines of his body in jeans and a fresh, dark shirt. Her spirits sank.

"Paco here wants to know if he can have a ride in the Cessna," she explained quietly.

Judd arched one brown and looked solemnly down at the young boy. He said something in rapid, expert Spanish and Paco's face fell in disappointment. Honor realized Judd must have refused the ride. But the conversation went on for a few more minutes, the language too rapid for her to understand completely. In the end Paco left with an expectant grin on his dark features.

"What did you tell him?" Honor asked as she shut the door behind her small visitor.

Judd shrugged. "That I didn't have enough fuel to take all the kids in the village joyriding and that if I did it for Paco I'd have to do it for the others. He understood and we compromised."

"Compromised?" Honor made her way across the small room to where the electric hot plate sat on a shelf.

"I agreed to let him and the other kids take turns sitting in the pilot's seat this afternoon. He's gone off to tell the others."

Honor smiled with sudden, unexpected gratitude. "Oh, Judd, that's very nice of you. Thank you. The kids will love that."

He eyed her mouth, not quite knowing what to

make of the smile. "It's no big deal. I don't mind since it looks like I'm going to be stuck here for two wasted days anyway." He could have kicked himself as soon as the words were out of his mouth. The dazzling, apparently genuine smile she was giving him disappeared instantly and the warmth that had momentarily lit her eyes was gone as if it had never been. It was replaced by the now-familiar wariness.

"Yes," she agreed in a grim little voice. "You will be stuck here for two wasted days, won't you?"

There was a small silence while she began heating a tiny skillet over the hot plate. Honor sensed that he was searching for another topic of conversation and the fact that he was temporarily at a loss for words was unaccountably satisfying.

"Paco seemed to like you," Judd finally remarked. He swung around one of the two straight-backed wooden chairs in the room and straddled it backward, his arms resting on the top.

Honor lifted one shoulder dismissingly. "I pay an outrageous sum for fresh eggs. I also pay well for fresh tortillas and fresh vegetables. Nothing like having money in a poor town to make one popular!"

"Or very unpopular," he retorted wryly. There was another pause and then he remarked laconically, "Everyone I've talked to for the past week who remembered you seemed to like you. They all spoke enthusiastically of the polite lady with the beautiful smile."

"I guess I have the bulk of the Mexican population fooled, haven't I?" she retorted bleakly, concentrating on the eggs while she heated two tortillas on the side of the hot plate. "Too bad everyone I've met hasn't had the opportunity to discuss my character failings with my loving family. Tell me something, Judd. How did you convince all those nice people to tell you about me?"

"I gave them an explanation they could comprehend very easily."

"I'll bet. What was it?" She dished out the eggs onto two chipped pottery plates and added a corn tortilla to each.

"That you were my woman who had run away and that I'd come to find you and take you home," he told her very casually, accepting one of the plates.

"So that's why Paco kept calling you my man." Honor sighed, having guessed as much. "What a joke."

He expertly curled the tortilla and used it to scoop up a section of egg. "If it's any consolation everyone seemed to be on your side."

"Then why the hell didn't they refuse to tell you where I was?" she snapped in annoyance.

"They wouldn't dream of interfering in a domestic situation of that sort," he drawled as she took the other straight-backed chair and began to eat in short, angry bites. "They all recognize the elemental fact that a man has certain rights over his woman."

"Uh-huh. So how did you get the impression they were on my side?" she demanded bitterly.

"Nearly everyone I talked to urged me not to beat you too severely when I eventually located you. They all seemed to feel you were just a high-strung, temperamental female who needed a gentle hand, not a heavy one."

Honor made a small, disgusted sound and downed another bite of egg and tortilla. "It looks like Mexico wasn't such a good choice as a hiding place, was it?

Maybe I should have tried Canada." Except that there she wouldn't have had the language barrier to slow down the two men who were hunting her. For all the good that had done her in the end, she thought sadly. They had simply hired someone who spoke Spanish to come after her.

Judd made no immediate response to her rhetorical comment. He wasn't about to tell her how strange it had seemed to pretend to everyone he met that she was his errant woman. He didn't want her to know about the times he'd been alone in the Cessna between villages when reality and fantasy had begun to merge; about the times he'd begun to wonder what the hunt would have been like if she actually were his runaway bride. The last time someone had advised him not to beat Honor too severely he had found himself nodding gravely and agreeing to accept the advice. The old man who was giving it had been pleased, smiling toothlessly and clapping him on the shoulder.

"You will see, my son," the old man had said cheerfully. "It will be worth your while to go easy on her. She has spirit and a good heart. A wise man does not break the spirit or harden a softhearted woman. Not if he knows what's good for him."

By the end of the week Judd was asking himself over and over again just what sort of woman he was hunting. Could she really fool so many people? Possibly. Look what she'd managed to accomplish last night. She'd wrangled a promise of two days' grace out of him—and that was after she'd pointed a gun at him and gone for his eyes with her nails. Automatically his fingers went to the angry red line on his cheek.

"I think," he said softly, "that it's time you started

feeding me the great fairy tale. I'm ready to listen now."

Honor stiffened resentfully and then reminded herself to take it one step at a time. After all, by rights she should have been stuffed into the Cessna this morning and halfway back to Arizona by now. One step at a time.

"It's not a long story, really, but the basic fact, the one I can't prove here in this village, is that the two men who hired you aren't related to me in any way. Their names are Leo Garrison and Nick Prager and they want me back so that they can silence me."

"You're going to stick by the paranoia theme?" Judd asked caustically, finishing his tortilla and egg combination.

"You said you'd listen with an open mind!"

"Have you got the makings for coffee?"

Honor subsided with a groan. "Yes. Instant. Be sure to boil the water well first. I've been lucky so far. I'd just as soon not get any intestinal problems now."

"Don't worry." He ran water from the bathroom sink, the only source, into a pot and set it on the burner. "Go on with the story. I promise not to interrupt again." But please don't make it totally impossible for me to believe, he found himself pleading silently as he put the water on to boil. Hell. Why was he thinking along those lines? He had no real intention of believing her in the first place. She was merely a job and he badly needed the two grand she would bring. Think of her as a couple of thousand on the hoof, he instructed himself bleakly. A pretty little mare he'd roped and was going to sell.

No, not a mare. That analogy reminded him too

vividly of the advice of one of the Mexicans he had talked to during the search. "Treat her as you would a gentle, spirited mare, son, and you won't go wrong."

Did gentle, spirited mares ever point guns at people?

Honor sat for a moment, moodily gathering her thoughts into the most logical sequence. Two days wasn't much time to convince a man like this of anything, let alone to talk him into leaving her behind in Mexico when he'd contracted to take her back to the States.

"All right," she began grimly, "here it is in a nutshell. Leo Garrison is undoubtedly the one who told you he was my father. I can see how he'd be very convincing. Used to be in the foreign service, you know. An embassy type. And he looks the part, too. Tall, distinguished, with all that snowy white hair and those wise blue eyes. And all that charm he honed to a fine point on the embassy cocktail circuit. He's the kind of man people like and trust on sight. I can't blame you for believing everything he told you. I once believed in him implicitly, myself. He assumed a fatherly role toward me right from the start . . ."

"From the start of what?" Judd asked dryly, watching the pot.

Honor frowned uneasily. "From the time I first went to work for him, of course. That was a year ago. He runs a very sophisticated, very expensive service for U.S. companies who want to do business in Asia and who don't know their way around that part of the world. Garrison served in Asia and Southeast Asia when he was working for the government. He spent twenty years as a respected embassy official, and during that time he made countless contacts with local businessmen and politicians. It was part of his job," Honor explained with a shrug.

"And after he left the foreign service he capitalized on those contacts?"

At least he didn't look too skeptical yet, Honor assured herself as she surveyed Judd from beneath her lashes. Of course, she hadn't yet told him anything unbelievable.

"That's right. U.S. companies operating abroad often don't know the first thing about doing business in a foreign country, especially an Asian or Southeast Asian country. Customs, politics, ways of doing business are all radically different and if you accidentally offend someone you can screw up a multimillion-dollar deal in thirty seconds. It pays to hire someone like Garrison to smooth the way and to advise on how to tiptoe through the masses of foreign red tape. It's a legitimate line of work, you understand," Honor added quickly. "There are several small, exclusive firms that offer that kind of service in various areas of the world."

"You're telling me you worked for Garrison?"

Honor nodded. "At the time I thought it had to be the most fabulous job I'd ever get. I was an assistant in the home office in Phoenix handling clients, acting as a liaison between Garrison and Prager. Nick was Garrison's partner." She paused, remembering in dismay how excited she had been at the prospect of working in such an exotic, romantic sort of business. The possibility of world travel and the opportunity to meet fascinating people had seemed so wonderful.

"Go on," Judd prompted softly, pouring the water into two cracked cups. He didn't look at her. Honor wondered desperately how much of her tale he was buying.

"Well, as I said, I worked in the home office, coordinating things between Garrison and Prager and the clients. Nick and Leo were constantly traveling. About three months ago Nick said he'd talked Garrison into letting me accompany them on some of the trips. I was thrilled! Couldn't believe my good luck. The first trip was to Taiwan and the second—" She broke off, remembering the second trip all too clearly.

"The second?" Judd prompted in a depressingly neutral tone as he handed her a cup.

"The second was to Hong Kong," she explained dully. She had left on that trip with such a romanticized view of both Nick and the business. The shattering of the illusion had been acutely painful, physically and emotionally.

"Why did Prager convince Garrison to take you along?"

She glanced at him sharply and then looked away. "Nick and I were seeing each other whenever he was in Phoenix. He wanted me with him." How much of this was Judd going to believe?

"A long-distance romance?" Judd asked derisively.

"Damn it! You said you wouldn't interrupt!"

"Just trying to get the story straight." But that hard, unreadable expression in his eyes didn't give Honor any clue as to whether or not he really was buying a single sentence of her tale. "Were you sleeping with him, then?"

"No, as a matter of fact, I was not sleeping with Nick," she told him tightly. "But we were becoming very close . . . Never mind. At any rate, I was elated at the idea of traveling. Taiwan was a fantastic experience and I got a chance to see how Garrison and Prager worked abroad. They're both consummate businessmen. They know the ins and outs of doing business in that part of the world like the back of their hands. And they have an incredible number of friends and contacts. I was very impressed. Then came Hong Kong."

"I sense the punch line coming up," Judd growled.

"Hong Kong," Honor explained very carefully, "was where I learned that in addition to their legitimate work Nick and Leo were into an interesting sideline."

"Which was?"

"Gunrunning. They buy and sell illegal arms all over that part of the world. Their regular business makes an excellent cover and provides them with countless contacts. It was my bad luck to stumble into the middle of a transaction involving several crates of automatic rifles and small arms."

"You just *stumbled* into the middle of such a deal?" Judd asked wryly as he sipped the strong coffee he had made.

Honor bit her lip as she realized how wild the whole thing must sound to him. "Leo and Nick had left me alone at the hotel while they supposedly went out one evening to a business dinner. While they were gone an important call came in from one of our best clients. He needed some information that I knew was in one of the files in the Hong Kong office. Eager to show my initiative and dedication I grabbed a taxi and rushed down to the office myself to get the information. Leo and Nick weren't due back until very late and I thought I'd impress everyone by taking care of the matter myself. Shows what initiative will do for a woman," Honor added caustically, remembering.

By now she had the horrible feeling she'd probably lost her audience entirely. Judd wasn't giving any outward indication of his reaction but she sensed his remote cynicism as if it were a tangible thing. There was nothing left to do but plow on with the story. In a flat, bleak tone she did so.

"I let myself into the building and went straight up to the third floor where Garrison and Prager had their offices. I was in the hallway just outside, about to insert my key in the lock, when I realized there was a light on inside and heard the sound of voices. It was the voices which scared me first. There was a terrible argument going on and I could hear Nick and then Leo. They were threatening a couple of other people. Something about a shipment that hadn't been paid for. The other voices claimed the rifles and small arms hadn't come with proper ammunition. Nick and Leo claimed that the others were lying and said they wouldn't okay delivery on the next batch of arms until the first had been paid for. I was terrified and shocked and in a panic. I knew I was overhearing far too much for my own good and that if Nick and Leo realized I was outside in the hall my life probably wouldn't be worth much. So I ran. As I started down the stairs I tripped. They must have heard the noise because by the time I reached the first floor I could hear them yelling on the staircase. As I dashed out into the street I heard Nick call my name. He was leaning out of the second-story window."

"What did you do?"

She could hear the disbelief in his voice. There was

no point going into all the details, reliving the terror of that horrible night. "I started running and I haven't stopped since," she said in a flat tone.

"But first you went home to Phoenix?"

She nodded. "I had to go home, but I knew I would be a sitting duck in Arizona. Nick and Leo would be able to take their time hunting me down on my own home ground. And who would listen to a wild tale like mine?" She broke off, remembering sadly that she had not even dared go to her own family with the story. The ironic part of this mess was that her parents' image of her was only a little better than the one Nick and Leo had fabricated. Had she approached them for help, her parents probably would have remembered the dreamy little girl who had woven exotic, romantic daydreams to amuse herself and wondered if Honor had slipped over the edge into some kind of permanent dream world. Pragmatic and down to earth, they had never understood her.

"How did you wind up here?" Judd asked matter-of-factly.

"As soon as I got home I grabbed the money from my bank account and packed a few things. Then I crossed the border into Mexico. Garrison and Prager don't have contacts in Central America. I figured I'd be safer here than anywhere else while I tried to decide what to do."

"And then I showed up last night," Judd concluded too easily. It was as if he were writing "The End" to the fairy tale she had just told him.

Honor nodded unhappily. "I knew as soon as I saw you that there weren't too many likely explanations for another tourist in this backwater village." Her fingers tensed painfully around the handle of her coffee cup. "I really thought I might have a chance here in Mexico. At least until my money ran out."

"Uh-huh. What were you going to do then?" he asked blandly.

"I don't know," she admitted despairingly. The truth was she hadn't been able to think that clearly as yet. "I suppose I'd hoped I'd eventually find someone who might pay attention to my story. I don't know! It's all been such a jumble and I've been frightened for so long. I decided I could stretch out my cash for quite a while. As you can see I'm not exactly living high on the hog!" She looked around the ramshackle room she'd been calling home.

"No, you're not, are you? How long would you have been content to live here, Honor? I should think you'd be grateful to me for coming along and taking you away from all this!"

Suddenly she was on her feet, the resentment and fear spilling over as she confronted him. "Don't make fun of me, damn it! It's obvious you don't believe me, but don't you dare mock me like that! It's my life that's at stake, you bastard! I can't help it if you're so damn pigheaded you bought that stupid story Garrison and Prager gave you. But mine is no wilder than theirs and I'm willing to pay you just as much to believe it. Since money is about all that seems to count with you, I should think you'd do me the courtesy of at least not laughing at me!"

"Are you going to assault me again?" he asked calmly, eyeing her clenched fists and angry eyes. Her slender body was drawn into a taut, furious line and she did, indeed, appear to be on the verge of throwing herself at his throat.

Honor decided against that, knowing in advance

that she didn't have a chance of defeating him physically. But his obvious unwillingness to give even an
ounce of credence to her story made some reaction on
her part inevitable. Her life was on the line, she told
herself in rage and panic, and this man was laughing at
her!

Without a second thought she hurled the contents
of her coffee cup into his face, the still-warm liquid
splashing out to douse his cheek and drip down onto
his shirt.

There was an electric silence as Judd's bird-of-prey
eyes burned into her stricken, defiant features. Honor
saw the attack coming before he had even moved,
instinct warning her that he would retaliate. She
swung on her heel and launched herself at the door.

She didn't even make it halfway across the tiny
room. Before she had gone two running strides Judd
was on her, reaching out to circle her waist with his
arm and yanking her back against the hard, taut
length of his body.

"Oh!" The small exclamation came as the force of
the impact made itself felt. She took a shuddering
breath. His arm was like a steel band around her and
there was no way on earth she could escape.

"If you can't get a reaction one way, you'll try
another. Is that it, Honor?" he demanded far too
gently. "Is that what you crave out of life? The
attention and reaction of every man who comes near
you?"

"Damn you!" she hissed helplessly, violently aware
of the way her softly rounded rear was being forced
against his thighs. The solid expanse of his chest was
like a brick wall behind her. Everything about this
man was like a brick wall, she told herself hysterically.

And somehow she had to find a way to climb it. Throwing her coffee in his face had probably not been an especially good technique for gaining his confidence, she decided in dismay and disgust. "I'm sorry, Judd," she tried awkwardly. "I lost my temper."

"And when you lose your temper you strike out at the nearest available victim?"

"I said I was sorry!"

"I think you're only sorry for your actions when they don't gain you what you want," he mused. Slowly he turned her around until she stood trapped in the circle of his arm, staring up at him in mute defiance. "What do you want from me, Honor?" he asked almost idly.

"I want you to go away and leave me alone. Go back to the States and tell Leo and Nick that you couldn't find me. I'll give you the two thousand you care so much about. Just go away and leave me here!"

"I can't do that. And throwing your morning coffee into my face isn't going to make me turn tail and run. Aiming guns at me in the middle of the night isn't going to do the trick, either. Trying to scratch my eyes out won't work and neither will telling me incredible adventure stories about illegal gunrunning. Last, but not least, bribery isn't going to work."

"Then what the hell will work?" she blazed. "What will it take to make you leave me alone, Judd Raven?"

"Probably nothing you've got to offer," he advised simply.

She whitened beneath the terrible finality of his words. Gamely she fought for her breath. "Then there can be nothing but war between us, Judd," she told him evenly. "As I told you last night, you'd better be prepared to cripple me or tie me hand and foot because I'm never going to stop fighting you."

He stared down into her wide hazel gaze as if searching for a hidden truth. The determination in her was evident in every rigid line of her body.

"Last night," he said deliberately, watching her face intently, "you tried to involve me in another kind of warfare. You practically dared me to take you. If I did that . . . if I put you down on the floor and stripped you naked and took you until you no longer had the strength or the will to go on fighting me, would that solve the problem? Would I still be obliged to knock you senseless or tie you hand and foot in order to control you?"

"You bastard!" she breathed. She was beginning to think he could do exactly as he said: throw her on the floor and force himself on her physically with no outward sign of emotion. That kind of dispassionate savagery was terrifying.

"I'm sure that in your eyes I probably am a bastard, Honor. But that's because you can't manipulate me. Or at least, not completely," he amended with a wry twist of his mouth. "The fact that I find myself spending two extra days in Mexico is evidence that you have some ability in that direction, isn't it?"

"That was a cold, hard cash deal, remember? Not manipulation. I'm paying you a thousand dollars a day to stay here!" She was beginning to hate the way he constantly accused her of manipulating people. "It's your own mercenary greed that is keeping you here in Mexico, Judd Raven!"

He considered that. "Not quite. I'd call it curiosity. I've been growing increasingly curious about you for a week, Honor. Now that I've found you I seem to be stuck with more questions than answers. And last night I went to sleep with one particularly large question on my mind. I found myself wondering what would have happened if I'd gone ahead and accepted your challenge."

"You mean what would have happened if you'd raped me?" she flung back.

"Are you sure it would have been rape, Honor?" he queried, as if only academically interested in the answer.

"What else could it be when a robot makes love to a woman?" she asked unwisely. "Go back to your airplane if you want someone who understands and appreciates what you're offering!"

He shook his head in disbelief. "Hell, lady, you just don't know when to stop pushing, do you?"

Then, before she quite realized his intent, he used his arm around her waist to draw her firmly against him. His other hand went to the back of her head, tangling in her unbound hair and holding her very still. For an instant longer he held her like that, reading the beginnings of pure, feminine fear in her eyes and watching the tiny tremor in her lips.

Quite lazily, as if he were only conducting some sort of experiment, Judd lowered his head and took her mouth.

This time there was none of the wild, enraged male lust she had endured the night before. This time there was absolute control, a kind of questing, searching quality in his kiss. Honor stood stock-still, partly because he was holding her immobile and partly because she couldn't have moved if she'd tried.

The sensation being generated in her was not easily defined. The initial fear hovered still in the back of her mind but it was rapidly metamorphosing into mere wariness. The dominant feeling she was experiencing was a strange, budding excitement, a new kind of hunger, and there was no way to explain it.

His lips moved languidly on hers, beginning to deliberately tease and tantalize until her mouth flowered open in a response Honor was helpless to control. She moaned softly at the moment his tongue slipped into the intimate warmth of her, and her fingers fluttered upward to rest against his chest, half in protest, half in desire. What on earth was happening to her?

"Judd, please, don't . . ." she breathed huskily when he slowly lifted his mouth from hers.

"You want rape instead?" he taunted softly. He lifted the hair off the back of her neck and pushed her face gently against his shoulder so that he could nibble at the delicate skin of her nape.

"No! Don't tease me like this," she wailed, her words muffled by his shirt. The touch of his lips on her nape was sending small shivers down her spine and her fingers clenched spasmodically into the hard line of his waist.

"I'm not teasing you, Honor," he muttered, his voice thickening as he touched his tongue to her ear. "I'm trying to get some questions answered."

"What questions!" she stormed unevenly and then realized she was leaning heavily against him as his hand trailed down her back to the waistband of her jeans.

"About what would have happened last night if I'd taken you there on the floor," he returned deeply. "Would you be soft and sweet in a man's arms, Honor Knight? Or would you be wild and maddening?"

"I'd probably be a lot less interesting to you than your damned airplane!" she rasped tightly.

He used his teeth a little roughly on her earlobe. "Honor, you're skating on thin ice at the moment. If you have any sense at all you won't continue trying to provoke me."

"Are you threatening me?"

"No, I'm making love to you, or hadn't you noticed?" His hands slid down to shape her buttocks and he propelled her audaciously into the cradle of his thighs. When he heard her small gasp he muttered something that sounded dark and satisfied.

Honor caught the blatantly masculine exclamation and it sent a ripple of new unease through her already tense body. "You're not making love to me, you're trying to teach me some kind of lesson," she accused wretchedly.

"I'm just curious about what I missed last night," he drawled.

"You didn't miss anything last night! I wasn't trying to get you to make love to me. Damn it! Will you stop deliberately misinterpreting what happened? Just let me go, Judd. Please. That's all I want. Just leave me alone."

He lifted his hands to cup her face, holding her so that she had to meet the hooded depths of his eyes. What she saw there alternately chilled and warmed her. He was quite capable of desire, she realized. It was there in his gaze, a dark male hunger that could never have been mistaken for anything else. But it was very much under control still. Honor caught her breath. She didn't understand this man, but she knew beyond a shadow of a doubt that he was far more dangerous than she had originally realized.

"Honor, I can't walk away and leave you here. You know that. I have a responsibility to get you back to Arizona. Why don't you just stop fighting me? You must know you can't possibly win."

"You didn't believe a word I said this morning, did you?" she whispered despairingly. "Not a single word."

"It was a rather bizarre tale," he pointed out almost gently.

She shut her eyes against the hopelessness of her situation and before she could open them again he was kissing her once more. She stood trembling beneath the increasing tension the kiss was generating in her, enduring the onslaught with an effort of pure will. How could she be on the verge of melting in the arms of the man who held her life in the palm of his hand? She must be as crazy, as certifiably crazy, as Leo and Nick had implied. Her reactions to Judd Raven made no other sense.

When Judd felt the unwilling softening of her body he lifted his head again to stare enigmatically down into her tortured eyes. "You want to make deals, Honor Knight? I'll make a deal with you. Stop fighting me. Come back to Arizona without a fuss and I'll stay with you until I know for sure that the man you call Leo Garrison is your father. That's the only compromise I'm willing to make, lady. Take it or leave it."

Honor clenched her teeth together against the frustration of it all. Didn't he see that by the time she could prove Leo wasn't her father it would probably be too late? For him as well as for her, if he insisted on accompanying her until she could provide proof.

"You can take your stupid idea of a compromise

and go straight to hell, Raven. Your way will get me just as dead as if I went back and threw myself on Leo's mercy," she spat out. With a small, violent little twist she jerked herself out of his arms and stepped backward.

"Honor, I'm trying to be reasonable about this," he began grimly.

"No, you're not. You're only trying to do things your way. Don't ask for your brand of reasonableness from me. I'll see you in hell before I get into that plane!"

"Or in bed," he amended speculatively.

Chapter 4

"I FEEL LIKE THE PIED PIPER," JUDD REMARKED LACONI-
cally an hour later as he opened the door of Honor's
small cottage and stepped out into the street.

From out of nowhere the children began to materi-
alize behind him as Judd walked Honor toward the
Cessna at the far end of the village. The little ones
must have been waiting and watching ever since
young Paco had spread the news about the promised
treat. In spite of her own predicament Honor felt a
tug on her emotions.

"These children have so little," she murmured as
the youngsters flocked around. "Getting to sit inside
an airplane will probably be the highlight of the year
for a lot of them."

Judd eyed the two or three barefoot kids who were
vying to catch hold of Honor's hand. "I wish . . ." he
began and then shrugged.

"Wish what?" Honor prompted.

"Oh, nothing. It would have been nice to have enough fuel to give them all a ride," he concluded. "But I don't, so that's that."

"Feel free to use your fuel on these kids," Honor shot back. "You won't need it for me!"

He gave her a slow, slanting glance. "Don't you ever stop fighting?"

"Not when my life is at stake! Would you?"

"Honor, be reasonable. That's the wildest story I've ever heard. Did you really expect me to believe it?"

"No," she admitted. "And I didn't expect the authorities to believe it, either. That's why I didn't go to them with it."

"Very wise," he drawled in mocking approval. "I'm sure you would have found the whole thing damned embarrassing."

Whatever Honor would have said next was cut off by the arrival of several adults. Some of the women hailed Honor with greetings that were half-sympathetic and half-amused.

"Buenos días, Honora," María Lopez said cheerfully, feminizing Honor's name with an "a" on the end as did most of the people Honor had encountered in the village. "Your man is very generous to take the children to the airplane. My Paco is so excited!" María spoke in slow, careful Spanish so that Honor could understand. Everyone in the village was so polite and patient with her poor Spanish, Honor thought fleetingly. But when they spoke to Judd they slipped into a more natural speech pattern and she couldn't always understand what was being said.

It was quite clear, however, that the villagers firmly

believed she belonged to Judd and that he had come
to collect her. Given his greater fluency in the language there was very little chance she would be able
to convince them otherwise. She didn't even know the
Mexican word for "kidnap"! Most of these people
seemed to believe she was exactly what Judd had
implied when he had asked about her the night
before. She was his runaway woman.

"Good morning, María," Honor said, managing a
small smile. "I hope Paco enjoys the plane."

"Sí, sí." María nodded enthusiastically, her brown
eyes smiling. Then she eyed Honor consideringly.

María Lopez wasn't the only woman in the small
crowd who was peering speculatively at Honor. Lupe
Martinez, Consuela Espinosa and several of the others were also casting interested gazes at the *Norte
Americana.* But no one said anything until the cluster
of men chatting with Judd effectively separated him
from Honor by a few feet. Then María leaned close.

"You are okay, hmmm? You look sad but you do
not seem . . ." She trailed off, searching for a word
Honor would recognize. In the end she gave up and
used one Honor didn't know.

"What?" Honor frowned intently, trying to comprehend. Instantly the other women began trying to
interpret. Their voices rose with their excitement and
Honor lost track of the conversation completely.
Helplessly she stared at one woman and then another,
trying to comprehend the chatter.

"They want to know how badly I beat you," Judd
explained, glancing back over his shoulder. "They say
you don't look happy but you don't look badly
bruised, either. They can't figure out why you aren't
looking more cheerful since you got off so lightly."

"You explain it to them!" Honor snapped, taking the villagers by surprise with the unexpectedly harsh tone of her voice. She glared across the heads of several of the women, who were generally shorter than she was, meeting Judd's dark eyes with cool challenge. "Go ahead. Explain why I'm not exactly thrilled to have *my man* show up and take me home!"

There was silence now as the adults around them glanced interestedly from one foreigner to the other. The children, losing patience, raced ahead down the street toward the waiting plane.

For a moment Judd regarded Honor's tense features and then he lifted one shoulder in casual dismissal of the vagaries of women and said something quickly in Spanish which brought a roar of laughter from the men and a series of knowing looks from the women. Then the whole group turned and started down the street again.

"What did you tell them?" Honor hissed, catching up to Judd.

"I explained that you weren't in a good mood this morning because, although I didn't beat you last night, I didn't make love to you, either."

"My God!" she breathed, incensed. "Isn't it enough that you're trying to kidnap me? Must you humiliate me on top of everything else?"

"Don't worry. If you find it so humiliating to have everyone in town know I didn't make love to you last night, I'll be glad to make up for it tonight."

"Bastard!"

He put a hand on her arm, bringing her to a sudden halt. When she automatically looked up into his face she saw the glittering eyes of the hunter and a chill trickled down her spine. "You've called me that more than once, Honor, and I'm getting tired of hearing it. Say it one more time and I really might resort to beating you."

"Ah, but that would necessitate losing your temper and I doubt you'd let your control slip that much."

"I haven't lost my temper in a long time," he murmured warningly. "It might be interesting to see what happens when I do. Are you sure you want to be the one standing in the line of fire, though?"

"It might be amusing to see another side of you besides the cold-blooded mercenary!" Which was a flat lie. Honor knew full well that genuine rage in this man would not be at all amusing. That brief flash of lust she had endured the previous night was warning enough that if Judd Raven ever did let himself go, his emotions might be violent. Was that why he had clamped such a tight lid on himself over the years? Did he fear the depths of his own passions?

"Honor, if I were the mercenary you claim I am I'd have taken your initial offer of a bribe and then returned you to the States and collected my fee on top of it," he pointed out as they started walking once more.

"As it is, you're going to collect the same amount without sacrificing any of your so-called business ethics, aren't you? Or were you planning on turning down the two thousand I'm offering for the two days you're spending here?"

"It occurred to me that since I didn't swallow your little story this morning, you might withdraw your offer of the two grand," he retorted dryly.

"What about you? Are you going to renege on your promise to spend the full two days here even though you have already decided not to believe me?" She tried to keep the anxiety out of her voice, but it was difficult. When she'd realized how hopeless it was going to be to convince him to believe her story she had immediately begun to wonder if he would grow impatient with the promise he had made. Two days wasn't much time but it was all she had.

"I told you I'd spend the two days here and I will. I don't break my promises, Honor."

For some reason Honor found herself believing him. He was a hard, cold man, she thought, but he was honorable in his own way. If only she could get him on her side! She had the distinct impression that, as an ally, Judd Raven would prove invaluable.

During the next hour and a half most of the population of the village took turns sitting in the Cessna, listening intently while Judd explained the instruments and controls, and generally playing make-believe. Judd was right, Honor decided as she watched the children as well as the adults thoroughly enjoying the small treat. It would have been nice to have been able to give everyone a ride.

It surprised her that he should even have mentioned the idea, though. Altruism didn't seem to have much place in the life of a loner like Judd Raven. The hour and a half spent guiding people through the plane wasn't easy on him, Honor realized. If she had been feeling in a more cheerful frame of mind she might even have found his controlled tension rather amusing.

The Cessna, as she had guessed the previous evening, occupied a very important place in his life and every time one of the children touched the controls with an overeager hand or clambered over the seats she could almost see Judd wince in pain. But he hid his anxiety well and he didn't cut the time short for anyone, not even the youngest. Still, when everyone had had his or her chance to play pilot and the door to the Cessna was firmly locked again, Honor could see the relief in Judd's face.

"Are you sure you don't want to sit in the pilot's seat, too?" he murmured as he double-checked the plane.

"No, thanks. I hate small planes and this one especially."

He cocked an eyebrow. "How about sitting in the pilot's lap, then?"

Honor blinked, taken aback by the hint of teasing in his voice. "If that's another attempt at a heavy-handed pass, forget it. I'm not interested in going to bed with the man who's going to get me killed."

He sobered at once, the faint trace of humor gone as if it had never been. "You are the most obstinate female I've ever met." He pocketed the keys and took her arm, following the rest of the crowd back into the village. "What would it take to make you quit playing this weird game, Honor?"

"A little trust on your part might do the trick."

"Can you blame me for being a bit short on trust? Your story is ludicrous, Honor. What I can't figure out is why you're sticking to it. The longer I know you the less I can buy the possibility that you're genuinely mentally ill."

"Well, that's a step in the right direction, I suppose." She sighed. "Is it going to change anything, though?"

"The fact that I'm more confused than ever by you? No, probably not in the long run." He hesitated and then said slowly, "But I might be willing to make one more compromise."

Stunned, Honor dug in her heels in the dusty road and tugged at his arm until he turned to look down at her. "What kind of compromise? What are you talking about?" The hope in her eyes was painfully evident. Judd couldn't have missed it if he'd tried.

"I might be willing to give you another day or two here in Mexico, Honor, on one condition."

"What condition?" she demanded suspiciously.

"That you'll stop fighting me every inch of the way. If you'll give me your word I won't have to tie your hands at night to avoid getting beaned with the frying pan. If you'll promise you'll stop accusing me of wanting to get you killed. Little things like that. How about it? Can you agree to those strenuous terms?" he growled.

"I'd probably agree to anything that delayed your efforts to get me back to Arizona," she admitted candidly. "Yes, I'll agree to your terms. How long do I have?"

"Say to the end of the week? We'll fly back on Saturday."

Saturday. He was adding two more days on to the original number for which she had bargained. Four days in which to try and establish some kind of trust between them. Honor smiled, her gratitude plain in her wide, hazel eyes. "Thank you, Judd."

He stared at her for an instant longer and then took her arm again. It was a hell of a price to pay for one smile of gratitude, he thought. What was the matter with him? Why couldn't he forget his curiosity and the strange attraction he was experiencing for Honor

Knight? She would be furious if she knew that the real reason he had elected to extend his stay in the village was simply because he wanted to indulge himself, not her.

It was stupid. There was no logical justification for his impulsive decision to give her an extra two days in Mexico. Now he was committed to four whole days in this remote village. It was an idiotic thing to do. He should be getting the job over and done and returning home to New Mexico. He had other work to do.

Well, it was too late to back out of the promise. That single smile of gratitude was probably all he was going to get by way of thanks, too. But damn it! It was infinitely more pleasant to have her smile at him than to see the anger and fear in those huge hazel eyes.

Then Judd corrected himself. Yes, it was very pleasant to see the smile, but what really intrigued him now was the possibility of seeing passion come to life in her eyes. He had managed to arouse some spark in her this morning and his whole being longed to know what the flame would be like if he could kindle it fully.

"That's the third compromise you've gotten out of me, lady. Are you satisfied?" he asked almost whimsically as they reached her cottage.

"Are you telling me you think you've been a very generous man?" she asked, throwing herself down onto the cot and folding her arms behind her head. She watched as he moved across the room to put on more hot water for coffee. Today her bird of prey had shown another side to his nature and she was still trying to assimilate it. His patience with the local people as he showed them over the Cessna and his surprising offer to grant her extra time both provided a great deal of food for thought.

"You sound as if you don't think I'm capable of generosity," he remarked, not looking at her as he measured coffee into the cups. He added an extra spoonful to his own and Honor winced at the thought of how strong it would be.

"Frankly, when I first saw you last night I wouldn't have bet so much as a dime on the possibility of your having a generous streak in your nature. I decided almost at once that your name fit you very well."

"Raven?" That brought a faint look of satisfaction to the line of his mouth. "I'll take that as a compliment. Ravens are good in the air, you know. There's not another bird that can bring them down in the sky."

"Is flying your whole life, Judd?" Honor asked impulsively. "Have you always made your living at it?"

"Ever since I got my license when I was sixteen. Crop dusting, charter work, ferrying, you name it."

"Do you often take on odd jobs like this one?" For some reason Honor chose to refrain from using the word "kidnap" to define his present employment. She found she didn't want to break the fragile truce that was developing between them. There was no telling just how far his generosity really went, after all.

"When I need the money."

"What do you need the money for this time?" she prodded.

He brought the coffee over to her. "You're full of questions all of a sudden."

"Natural under the circumstances, don't you think?" she asked flippantly.

"Maybe," he said slowly. "Maybe it is. Perhaps that explains why I've got so many questions about you. When you've spent a solid week hunting a woman, you're bound to be a little curious about your quarry."

She made a face. "If you don't mind, could you find some word other than 'quarry'? It's not pleasant feeling like a hunted animal."

"Then why did you run away in the first place?" he countered too gently.

She stiffened. "I thought we had agreed not to make accusations. Asking me that is tantamount to calling me a liar again. You don't believe a single word of my story, do you?"

"Let's try another topic," he suggested coolly.

"Such as?"

"Such as, will you have dinner with me in the cantina tonight?"

That came as a surprise and Honor blinked, appraising him from beneath her lashes. It was another small step forward on his part and she intended to seize the gesture with open arms. But that didn't stop her from wondering exactly what was going on behind those cool, dark eyes. Until she fully understood his motives, Honor was nervous about drawing any conclusions from the various small victories she seemed to be winning.

Was he really beginning to melt toward her? Perhaps that kiss this morning had elicited more than just a physical response in him. The unquenchable flame of hope began to glow within her again. There was still a chance of convincing Judd Raven to see things from her side. He was offering time and even a measure of protection. That was a long way from trust, of course, but she would work with what she had.

"I'll be glad to have dinner with you, Judd," she said very politely, just as if he were inviting her out on a real date. Then she risked a smile, one that reached her eyes. "Do you think you can manage to refrain from telling everyone in the cantina about your techniques for dealing with an errant wife?"

"If you refrain from challenging me in front of the villagers, I'll be able to keep my mouth shut about how I plan to bring you to heel," he said blandly. Too blandly. "But be warned. A man has to keep his woman in hand."

Honor eyed him wonderingly. Was Judd trying to tease her again? She simply didn't know how to take this man. "Have you been pretending all week that I'm your wife?"

"It was the simplest way to get people to talk about you," he said quietly.

"Effective, too," she muttered dryly. "There's no way I could make any of these people around here believe that you have no right to take me back to the States."

"No," he agreed, sipping his coffee. "There isn't."

The finality of the words washed away her lightened mood. "It would serve you right if you had a real wife who took offense at your little game!" she snapped, rolling off the bed and getting to her feet.

"How do you know I don't have a real wife?" he asked, sounding rather curious.

Honor was pulling clothes out of her pocket-sized closet. How did she know he wasn't married? Good grief! Wasn't it obvious? "I knew it the minute I saw you last night. You're a loner, aren't you, Judd?" She collected a few more items from her suitcase, which served as a dresser drawer. "It's in your eyes. It's all over you. You go through life alone and you like it that way. Except for your plane, naturally," she added too sweetly. "I guess it's sort of like a cowboy and his horse, isn't it? Remember those old pictures in which the cowboy hero kisses his horse . . . Judd!"

She leaped back, her arms full of clothes as he came across the room with sudden violence. Honor found herself with her back against the wall of the cottage, staring up at a man who clearly didn't intend to take any more.

"One more crack about me making love to my airplane and I'll show you in no uncertain terms that I haven't completely forgotten how to deal with a real life female!" he rasped, his fingers closing lightly around her throat. The raven eyes gleamed down at her and the expression in them caused Honor's mouth to go dry.

"Isn't it true that you care more about that plane than you do most people?" she dared.

He released her throat, pulling his hand away with deliberate caution as if the temptation to strangle her might still overcome him. "You just never give up, do you?"

But he was once more under control and Honor slowly relaxed. "I'm sorry, Judd. It's been a bit rough lately. I'm not at my gracious, scintillating best these days. I suppose I should be grateful to have someone else around with whom I can speak English!"

He frowned. "Has it been lonely for you, Honor?"

"Everyone in the village is very nice but I'm not really one of them and the language barrier makes involved conversation difficult." Honor started toward the door with the load of laundry in her arms. "Yes, I've been lonely. Unlike you, I like to have friends around occasionally. Friends I can talk to. People who trust me and whom I can trust."

She was almost through the door when he said quietly behind her, "You can trust me, Honor."

That stopped her. She turned to look at him over her shoulder, eyes narrowed. "Maybe. In your own hard, cold way, you probably are trustworthy. But you don't trust me, so it's all pretty hopeless, isn't it?"

"Damn it to hell, what do you want from me?" But she was already through the door and he was forced to follow. "Honor, wait. Where are you going with those clothes?"

"To the local laundromat." She kept walking, heading toward the western side of the village. A wide stream flowed along the boundary of the village and there were already a number of chatting women at work doing the family laundry. Honor joined them, rolling up her jeans and stepping into the cool, clear water to do her weekly wash.

On the ridge of ground above the stream Judd stood watching as Honor rinsed her clothes in the water along with the other women. The villagers greeted her happily, calling out her name and teasing her about the tall, dark man who stood on the bank. Judd knew Honor didn't fully understand most of the teasing remarks or she probably would have been furious. Still, she must have caught the essence of the women's meanings because her face was flushed and it wasn't just from bending over to wash her underwear.

On an impulse he turned around and walked back to Honor's shack. In his overnight bag he located two of the shirts he had worn during the week and started back to the stream. Deliberately he walked down to the water's edge and called softly.

"Honor?"

She glanced up warily, holding a soaking-wet pair of panties in one hand. For a moment Judd found himself oddly distracted by the sight of the feminine garment. Unbidden, a vision of Honor wearing only the silky underwear came into his head and he found himself swallowing awkwardly. Why did he suddenly feel so warm?

"Honor," he tried again, "would you mind doing these shirts? I could use some fresh clothes. Especially if we're going out tonight."

She stared at him as the women around her giggled delightedly. They might not have understood his English but there was no doubt about what he was asking his woman to do.

Then she proceeded to shock her audience by demanding in simple Spanish, "What will you give me, *señor,* in exchange for washing your shirts?" She tilted her head saucily, her hands on her hips, as the village women gasped in dismay at the utter daring of Judd Raven's woman. Didn't she know when she was well-off? She had been lucky enough to get away without a beating for the grave crime of running away from her husband, and now she seemed determined to push her luck. Crazy *Norte Americana.* Everyone waited in breathless anticipation to see what Judd would do. Just imagine, a woman demanding payment for doing her husband's laundry! It was incredible.

"She will get payment, all right," Lupe Martinez confided to her friend María. "She will get a taste of his belt! That one is not a man to put up with her sauciness!"

"He has yet to beat her," María pointed out practically. "Perhaps he won't this time, either. But I think she will do his shirts in the end."

Judd stood quietly for a moment contemplating Honor's unexpected sassiness. Somehow he'd just assumed she'd take the damn shirts and do them without a fuss. After all, she was already wet.

He tried to read her expression. She didn't look angry or even rebellious. What sparked in her green-and-gold eyes was closer to outright mischief than anything else. It confused him. Anger or rebellion he could handle. How did a man deal with a woman bent on mischief?

"What do you want in exchange for washing the shirts?" he finally hedged, speaking in English.

"How about an autographed picture of you kissing your plane?"

He stared at her, hardly able to believe his ears. Wasn't she ever going to let up on that idiotic business with the plane? Damn it to hell! How did she dare to taunt him like this in front of the village women? Even if they didn't understand what she had said they knew perfectly well a challenge had been issued.

"I'm beginning to think you're jealous of the Cessna," he drawled coolly.

She tossed her head. "You ought to be careful about putting all your faith in that metallic female. My guess is she has a heart of ice-cold steel. Of course, that might suit a man like you to perfection."

"Is your heart any softer or warmer?" he asked evenly.

That brought a flush to her cheeks but she held her ground, standing ankle-deep in the stream, her hands on her hips. "Only for the right man!"

"Which, I assume, isn't me?" He arched one black brow inquiringly.

"You assume correctly," she told him with relish.

"Well, then, if your heart is as cold as the Cessna's, there's not much difference between the two of you, is there?" Why the hell was he standing there letting her bait him like this? But he was trapped, Judd knew. He couldn't walk away from the challenge. Even if there hadn't been any witnesses he wouldn't have been able to walk away from it. The need to answer Honor Knight's saucy defiance was almost primitive. He felt a desire to assert himself over her that he couldn't fully explain. The shirts were rapidly becoming only an excuse. What had gotten into him?

"Oh, I'd say there are still a few differences between me and that damned plane," Honor said cheerfully, beginning to feel on top of the situation.

"Name one," he growled.

"I can dance."

He nodded as if taking that fact into consideration. "Can you?"

"Ummm. And I can broil a steak."

"A useful talent."

"Let's see, what else? I can mix a good margarita."

"If you're that skillful with your hands I'll bet you can wash these shirts, too."

"I probably could. If they happened to belong to a man who preferred me to an airplane. But since they don't . . ."

But Judd, apparently, had had enough. Amid the

excited squeals of the women he leaned down and yanked off his boots. Then, heedless of the fact that his jeans were getting wet around the bottom edges, he started forward into the stream.

On a note of laughing protest, Honor turned and ran, heading for the opposite bank. A part of her delighted in having provoked him with her teasing. He wasn't truly angry this time, merely determined to win the small confrontation. She wasn't even sure but what, in some small way, he was actually enjoying himself, although she had the feeling he would never admit it. This kind of playfulness was new to him, she realized, and he didn't quite know how to deal with it.

Which didn't mean he wasn't going to make a damn good try, she acknowledged as he came striding across the stream toward her.

"Judd! No, wait . . . !" she gasped, torn between laughter and an unexpected panic as he leaped onto the bank behind her and scooped her up in his arms. "I was only teasing." She felt the strength in him as he carried her easily against his chest back into the stream. There was a sensuous, blatantly erotic tug on her senses as she absorbed the impact of his sun-warmed body. "What are you going to do?" she demanded, trying and failing to struggle free. Around her the other women laughed delightedly.

"Get my shirts washed."

Damn it! She still couldn't read the expression in his eyes. Was he amused? Or was he simply set on getting his shirts washed? What was it with this man? Couldn't he give vent to any of the softer emotions like playful humor?

"Judd?" Suddenly she started to lose her nerve.

She didn't understand this man and it was dangerous to tease wild animals. She should never have started the mischievous byplay.

"Pick up the shirts, Honor," he ordered in a deep, dark voice as he reached the opposite bank with her in his arms. He stood in the water and lowered her just far enough so that she could reach the two shirts he had left lying on the ground.

Feeling more uncertain than ever now, Honor did as ordered, reaching down to collect the two shirts. As soon as she had them in her hands he straightened and carried her back into the middle of the stream.

"Judd, put me down," she commanded quickly as a premonition told her what he planned to do. The stream became wider and deeper just a few feet away. Deep enough to toss in a recalcitrant woman together with two shirts that needed washing! "Judd, so help me, if you—"

The rest was lost as Judd found the spot he was looking for and opened his arms. With a resounding splash Honor sank below the surface of the stream, automatically clutching the shirts that had been in her hands.

Damn it to hell, she thought furiously as she floundered for a moment beneath the surface. You'd think a grown woman would have known better than to taunt a wild, unpredictable bird of prey.

She came back into the air, standing waist-deep in the stream, and found her tormentor watching from a short distance away. He was only in water up to his calves.

"Are the shirts done yet?" he asked politely in Spanish. The women shouted their laughter, vastly amused by the whole scene. The *gringos* were crazy, but they livened up the place.

Honor glared at him, her hair dripping in a sleek, wet mass around her shoulders. She honestly didn't know whether to be elated or infuriated. She certainly didn't appreciate the high-handed treatment, even if she had brought it all on herself. By rights she ought to be feeling outraged.

But there was a gleam in Judd's dark eyes that was totally new. A playful, almost human expression which told her that in the end he had been playing with her, not just manhandling her.

It was one of the few cracks she had seen in that wall he had built around himself and it was strangely reassuring. Laughter could form a bond, too, just as other emotions did.

Four days. Four more days in which to get him to trust her. Getting dunked was a cheap price to pay for having opened a tiny chink in the wall. Her life depended on demolishing every last brick.

"I do believe your shirts are about finished," she informed him in careful Spanish for the benefit of their audience. "If you'll give me a minute longer I'll see that they get properly rinsed."

She wasn't sure she had the right word for "rinsed," but everyone seemed to know what she meant. It was fairly obvious she had temporarily surrendered to the will of her lord and master, Honor thought wryly. Across the stream Lupe and María giggled.

Judd stared for a moment as Honor bent to scrub the two shirts. He was aware of a fierce satisfaction at having won the small, meaningless battle. In addition to the satisfaction there was an undeniable feeling of pure, masculine pleasure in watching Honor wash the damn shirts. He liked to see her touching his things and know that he would be wearing them later.

What was the woman doing to him? How the hell did he come to find himself standing fully clothed in a stream watching Honor Knight do his laundry?

Honor kept her head submissively bent, devoting great attention to the shirts. But her mood was lighter than it had been since Judd Raven had arrived in town.

The hunting bird Leo and Nick had sent after her had a human side to his nature. She'd seen it this morning when he'd let the whole village take turns sitting in his precious airplane. And she'd seen it again this afternoon as he found himself engaged in a playful game of taming the shrew.

She had four days to turn the bird of prey into a man who could trust her.

Chapter 5

TWO DAYS LATER HONOR'S HOPEFUL DETERMINATION TO create a bond between herself and Judd was faltering badly.

The problem, she told herself in disgust, was that the man was a slow learner. An emotional underachiever. Furthermore, unless he was answering a direct question his conversation tended to be rather limited. The one exception was when she asked him questions about his flying. He opened up slowly but surely on that topic. Unfortunately it wasn't a topic that furthered her goal.

Oh, she was making progress on one front. As she had discovered that afternoon at the stream, Judd could be provoked into something resembling playfulness. It was, she freely admitted, somewhat like trying to play with an untamed, unpredictable wild creature, but it *was* a form of genuine playfulness. He never actually laughed, but once or twice a smile had actually touched his mouth and his eyes. It was as if he himself wasn't very certain of his own emotional state on those occasions when she provoked him with teasing banter or challenge.

On another front she was having far less success. During the two days that had passed since her dunking in the stream, she had made any number of efforts to get Judd to talk about himself. It was like talking to a clam.

"It must be a nice, simple sort of life for you," she finally exploded one night over drinks in the cantina. "No emotional involvement, no having to take chances on people, no need for socializing. Tell me something, Judd Raven. Have you ever fallen in love?"

"No."

The monosyllabic answer stopped her for a few seconds. She stared at him in utter disbelief. "Never? In your whole life? My God, you must be nearly forty years old!"

"You don't have to look at me as if I've suddenly grown two heads."

"But never to have fallen in love in your whole life . . ."

He glared at her. "I didn't say I haven't had a few interesting affairs, damn it! Why are you always trying to make it sound as if I'm not capable of going to bed with a woman?"

"I'm not talking about sex. I'm talking about a serious relationship!" she retorted. "There's a difference, you know!"

"Is there?"

"Oh, for crying out loud!" Honor exclaimed in

absolute disgust, sinking back into her chair and snatching up her margarita.

Judd studied the rigid line of her eyebrows and the sulky twist of her mouth and then he astounded her by asking, "Have you?"

"Have I what?" She didn't bother looking at him, concentrating instead on the row of men at the bar.

"Have you ever been seriously involved with a man?" he asked patiently.

For an instant she didn't know what to say, and then she decided on the truth. Perhaps he really was trying to make meaningful conversation. She didn't want to throw cold water on his efforts. "A couple of times," she admitted cautiously.

"When?"

Why was he suddenly so interested? Well, far be it from her to squelch the first heart-to-heart talk they'd had yet. "There was a man in Phoenix," she began hesitantly, thinking of Steve Melbourne with his three-piece suits and his easy, sophisticated charm. "We had a lot in common. Both of us had careers in the business world, we enjoyed the same things. He was very handsome," she added lamely.

"So what went wrong?" Judd demanded.

Honor glared at him. "Nothing went wrong. We just decided we weren't right for each other, that's all." How could you explain a relationship that had seemed to have everything going for it but somehow lacked the magic? There had never been any flash of boundless excitement between herself and Steve Melbourne, no matter how hard she had wished for it. Everything had seemed so right on the surface, but her romantic soul had shied away from a relationship that totally lacked passion. It was not, Honor had sadly learned, a commodity that could be infused at will into an association between a man and a woman. It was either present from the beginning or it was completely lacking.

"Do you still see him?" Judd pressed stonily.

"We're friends." She shrugged. "He's engaged to someone else now, but, yes I still see him occasionally."

"Friends! Then you couldn't have been in love with him," he declared flatly. "No man who'd ever been involved with you in a love affair could remain friends with you after it was over!"

"You're an authority on the subject?" she drawled, fiercely resentful of his certainty.

"I'm just stating the obvious. Tell me about the other times you were in love. You said there had been a couple of occasions."

"Is this just morbid curiosity on your part or genuine interest?"

"Just tell me, okay? It was your idea to talk about this."

"The second occasion was a bit more dramatic. It nearly got me killed!" she retorted without pausing to think. He was annoying her now with his persistent questioning of her love life.

"Almost got you killed? Oh, Prager."

"Yes, Prager." She looked down at her drink, morosely stirring it with a finger. She suddenly didn't want to talk about Nick at all.

"You told me before that you were carrying on a long-distance romance. You might as well give me the whole dazzling story," he mocked gruffly.

Was anything being accomplished with this? Honor

wondered unhappily. "Nick and I were becoming very close. He hired me into the firm and right from the start we were interested in each other. I suppose he seemed very romantic to me with his globe-trotting and all his connections. And he can be very charming," she admitted with a sigh. "He knows how to make a woman feel pampered. Special. I thought . . . I thought he loved me." She broke off, shivering at the memory of how quickly Nick's love had turned into a chilling threat. The man knew how to create the kind of mood that had appealed to her sense of the romantic, and she had been fool enough to respond to it. That trip to Hong Kong would have been the setting for the true beginning to their love affair if only Nick hadn't turned out to be another kind of man altogether. Honor shuddered again at the thought of how close she had been to going to bed with a man who had shown no compunction about trying to kill her.

"So far you've told me you've managed to get involved with a man with whom you're now 'friends' and another whom you claim wants to kill you. Hell of a track record, Honor. Only a woman with a vivid imagination could classify either of those two tales as love affairs! You must be one of the last of the great romantics. If you want my opinion all you've had are a few interesting affairs, just like me." Judd sounded utterly convinced of his own conclusions.

So much for the heart-to-heart exchange of confidences, Honor thought irritably. Time was running out and she still hadn't made much headway in winning over this lone hunter of a man. All she'd accomplished tonight was to make herself seem like some kind of empty-headed, romantic fool.

There was one other area in which Judd could be provoked into dramatic action, she knew, but ever since that devastating kiss, Honor had steered scrupulously clear of any attempt to elicit a sensual reaction from him. Oh, she still taunted him occasionally about his affection for the Cessna, but she never carried it far enough to make the situation dangerous.

She had known after that kiss that she was afraid to do so. It was that simple.

The possibility of using his physical attraction for her to build a sensual bond was too disturbing. Instinctively Honor sensed that, once started, she wouldn't be able to control the outcome.

Judd made no secret of his willingness to share her bed but he was still manageable. He was still sleeping on the floor and that was where Honor had decided to keep him.

His constant proximity, however, was having an effect on her nerves. At night she lay on the cot and watched his quiet form curled on the floor for a long time before she fell asleep. Sometimes she would awaken from one of the many dreams of loneliness and undefined fear she'd had since she'd begun her self-imposed exile and took a deep comfort from Judd's quiet presence in the room.

Which made absolutely no sense at all when she considered how dangerous he really was.

It wasn't until the third night of her four-day reprieve that desperation began to set in. Honor knew that although some communication was taking place between herself and Judd, it wasn't yet of a sufficiently bonding nature to assure her of his loyalty and trust. How could they build a relationship that intense when most of their conversations were about airplanes and flying? Besides, Honor thought in disgust, she was getting tired of always being the one to initiate the conversations! Judd didn't actually seem to mind talking, he just didn't seem to know quite how to get things started. His social life must have been rather limited, Honor mused grimly. He obviously hadn't had much practice in verbal communication. Probably stemmed from sitting too long alone in the cockpit of an airplane!

She knew she had been far quieter than usual herself that third afternoon. Her head had been filled with an examination of the few options left to her. She could try to sabotage the plane, although at best that would only be a delaying tactic and one that would surely enrage Judd. That damned Cessna was all he seemed to care about in the world. God help her if she crippled it badly.

Then there was the possibility of making a scene at the border when they landed to go through customs, assuming Judd didn't intend to try to sneak her back into the country by avoiding port of entry airports. But what if he did decide to avoid potential problems and simply flew her in illegally?

"Are you ready to go get a bite at the cantina?" Judd asked, interrupting her thoughts. It was almost six o'clock. They had spent the morning walking by the stream and like everyone else had stayed inside during the hot afternoon. Conversation between them had grown increasingly sparse as Honor exhausted her options. She was abandoning hope of communicating meaningfully on a verbal level.

"Yes, I'm ready." She followed him out into the

warm evening and together they walked down the street to the cantina.

"You're awfully quiet, Honor." Judd pushed open the door and led her to a familiar table. Across the room the older woman who ran the place waved a hand in greeting.

"I'm getting scared," Honor said simply.

He gave her a sharp glance. "Don't be frightened. I've told you I'll stay with you until we get the whole mess sorted out at the other end," he reminded her a little roughly.

She shook her head forlornly. "You just don't believe me, do you?"

"Let's say I'm reserving judgment at this point," he temporized.

She recognized that some progress had been made if he was no longer flatly denying the possibility that she'd been telling him the truth. But that wasn't going to do her much good. Honor smiled wanly. "By the time you satisfy yourself as to the truth of the matter it will be too late to do me much good. Judd, before you hand me over to Leo and Nick will you please give me back the bullets to my gun?"

He stared at her. "Hell, you're serious, aren't you? What's the matter? Don't you trust me to look after you in the event you're telling the truth?"

"How can I risk my neck in the hands of a man who doesn't trust me?" she asked bluntly, hazel eyes glittering with repressed anger and frustration.

"Honor . . . Forget it. Just forget it," he muttered and some of his own frustration and anger began to show through the wall of his self-control.

Was he really that upset about the situation? Honor wondered. If so it was the first indication she'd had that he might be experiencing some inner turmoil over the matter.

But there was so little time left. So little time.

The silence between them lengthened and Honor did nothing to terminate it. Normally she pushed the conversations, often initiating them and keeping them going when Judd became reticent. Tonight she made no effort and Judd didn't seem to know how to take over, although he tried a couple of times.

"Damn it, why aren't you talking to me tonight?" he finally demanded in something close to exasperation. "You're usually chatty enough! You've been getting quieter and quieter all day. Sulking?"

Honor blinked balefully, recognizing that the taunt was designed to draw some reaction from her. "I guess so. I'm just a spoiled, neurotic brat, remember? I've probably been too long away from my psychiatrist."

He glared at her and then abruptly threw some money down on the table. "Let's go. We've got a long day ahead of us tomorrow." Reaching down he snapped the beer, her third, out of her hand and yanked her roughly to her feet.

"Mr. Macho," she complained as he strode out of the cantina with her in tow. "Do you always treat your women like this?"

"Only when they've had one too many beers," he gritted, tugging her down the street toward the shack they shared.

"Surely even you wouldn't deny a condemned woman her last beer?" she taunted. "Or are you so cold and unfeeling that you'd do something that mean?" She wasn't drunk, but she was feeling a little light-headed with despair and panic. It was making

her reckless and desperate. This was her last night
with Judd. Her last chance to turn him from enemy to
friend and everything was going wrong.

The reaction to her taunt was more than she had
expected. Much more. Judd had let other, similar
remarks pass without much more than a verbal warning but tonight his self-control was not as firmly in
place as it usually was.

At least that was the only explanation Honor had
for what he did next.

"Damn it, Honor Knight," he rasped, jerking her
to a halt in front of her cottage and spinning her
around to face him. "That's enough out of you! I've
had it with your sharp little tongue, do you hear me?
You want to find out just how cold I am? I'll show
you!"

She had only time enough to recognize the masculine frustration and grim determination in him before
she was swept against his chest in a sudden, savage
embrace. "Earlier you accused me of not talking
enough!" she got out just before his mouth closed
over hers. "Now you're saying I've got a sharp
tongue. Make up your mind!"

His answer was to seal the remainder of the heated
protest deep in her throat. With grim intent he took
her mouth, folding her arms behind her back and
holding her helpless.

Honor sensed the will to dominate in him, but she
also was made violently aware of the depths of his
hunger. This wasn't the enraged, irrational lust she
had provoked the first night, nor was it the cold,
deliberate attempt at seduction which had comprised
his second kiss the other morning. Whatever this was,
it was real. Deeply sensuous, primitive and real.

The heat in him seemed to flow out to envelop her as he slowly and intently took command of her lips. She could feel the warmth emanating from the whole length of him and the strength in his arms seemed elemental and strangely reassuring.

He was going to make love to her tonight. Honor knew it now as surely as she knew the sun would rise tomorrow. There was nothing she could do to stop him and, heaven help her, nothing she *wanted* to do to stop him. The passion between them had been evident that first night, even though it had taken a violent form. Although she had tried to ignore it in favor of developing other avenues of communication, Honor had been aware of its existence from the start. And so had Judd, she decided. So had Judd. He wasn't as cold and unfeeling as she had accused him of being.

No man who was truly cold and unfeeling could be generating this level of sensual tension within her. On that thought her mouth opened under the impact of his and she heard the low groan of desire that came from deep in his chest.

As his tongue hungrily invaded the territory behind her lips Judd released her hands, which he had been holding captive behind her back. Shakily Honor moved her fingers to splay them against his hard chest and she moaned softly.

"Judd, oh, Judd . . . !"

"Hush, Honor. You wouldn't talk to me earlier and it's too late now." He used his teeth in an incredibly gentle, amazingly erotic caress against her throat and when she cried out in a tiny voice he slid his palms down the length of her back.

She felt her lower body being arched into his and shivered. There could be no doubt that he was aroused and waiting for her. The suddenness of his response brought to life another flicker of panic as Honor sensed her inability to control the situation and she pushed at his chest in an awkward protest.

"Don't fight me, Honor," he half pleaded, half ordered. "Put your arms around me and stop fighting me. Can't you see that I have to have you tonight?"

Before she could find an answer to that age-old question there was a good-natured hail from across the street as two of the cantina's patrons went past on their way home. Judd reluctantly lifted his head. The men asked him a quick, laughing question and he responded in the negative. Then he scooped Honor up into his arms and prodded open the door to her cottage with his foot.

"What did they say?" she asked uncertainly as he kicked the door shut behind him. "Something about waiting?"

"They asked if I couldn't wait until I could find a mattress on which to put you," he explained huskily. "I told them it would be very hard to wait even that long!"

"Judd!" She knew she was turning a dull shade of red and was grateful for the surrounding shadows.

"It's true," he told her heavily, carrying her across to the small cot. "I think I began wanting you when I was hunting you, pretending to be after my runaway wife. I knew for certain that I wanted you after that first night when you pulled the gun on me. Why do you think I've been willing to spend four extra days in this godforsaken village?"

She watched him in the moonlight as he settled her down on the cot and then sat down beside her. He meant it. He truly did feel something very strong for her. She could see it in the rigid cast of his features and in the hooded depths of his dark eyes. His fingers trembled slightly as they reached out to curve around the base of her throat.

Slowly he drew his hand from her throat down to the first button of her shirt. Honor lay perfectly still, her eyes never leaving his face as he undid the fastening.

"I don't know," she whispered huskily. "I'm not sure if this is the right way for us. But, oh, God! I don't know of any other way to find out what you really feel for me!" She caught hold of his fingers, staying them as they would have wandered down to the next button. Her eyes were wide with anxiety and the beginning flames of desire.

"Honor, I'm not much good with words. I've never been good with words. Let me show you how badly I want you. I need you tonight. Dear Lord! How I need you!"

He bent over her, feasting once more on her mouth. Gently he withdrew his hand from her restraining grip and finished unbuttoning the shirt she wore. He pushed aside the edges of the fabric and flattened his palm on her bare stomach.

"Oh, Judd." She sighed, lifting her arms to circle his neck. "I don't understand you. Not completely. But tonight—"

"Tonight doesn't need words," he muttered thickly against her mouth. "Just touch me, honey. I want you to touch me. I'm aching for you!"

His palm moved up from her stomach and shaped her breast. Honor heard his indrawn breath of satisfaction as the nipple beneath his hand instantly began to tighten. She hadn't worn a bra since she'd arrived in Mexico. The heat made such a garment uncomfortable. But the lack of it tonight left her feeling very vulnerable.

Or was it simply that Judd Raven's touch made her feel vulnerable? Whatever the reasons, there was no denying that her body was reacting fiercely to his lovemaking. Her breasts felt swollen and taut as he moved his palm slowly across the tips. A slow tendril of desire was uncurling deep in her loins.

"You feel so good," he breathed, burying his lips against her throat. "When you came up out of the water the other day in the stream your shirt was clinging to your breasts and I could see the outline of your nipples. It was all I could do not to reach out and take you right then and there."

She shuddered beneath the impact of his words and her body curved invitingly toward him. "Please, Judd . . ." Without a word he took her hand and guided it to the buttons of his own shirt. In slow, aching silence she began to undress him while he watched her face in the moonlight.

Once or twice during the mornings she had seen him bare from the waist up and had refused to allow her gaze to linger on the crisp, curling expanse of hair that covered his broad chest. But now, tonight, she could indulge herself to her heart's content. As she slipped the shirt from his shoulders Honor caught her breath at the primitive picture he made in the shadowy light.

"What is it, honey?" he murmured as she hesitated before touching him again. "What's wrong?"

"You frighten me a little, Judd. There are so many things we don't know about each other and you . . . can be very intimidating."

"I told you earlier not to be frightened. Of me or anything else." He unclasped his belt, standing up abruptly to finish removing his clothes. She watched the smoothly muscled, lean length of his body appear and felt a rush of painful awareness at the sight of his uncompromisingly aroused masculinity.

"You look as if you're on the verge of changing your mind, Honor," he said as he sat back down beside her. "You look as if you're having thoughts about running. But you can't run away now. You know that, don't you? I couldn't let you go tonight."

There was an absolute certainty in his words that told her he meant them. There was no way she could escape what had begun there in the small shack. And deep down Honor admitted to herself that she wouldn't have been able to run from him anyway. She felt overwhelmed and overtaken. There was no longer a choice to be made. It had been made the moment he had taken her in his arms.

As if he sensed her implicit surrender Judd lowered his head to kiss her breasts as his hand unzipped the fastening of her jeans. Impulsively reacting to the feel of his sensitive tongue on her aching nipples, Honor clenched her fingers into the raven darkness of his hair and cried out softly.

"Yes," he growled in return. *"Yes!"* Then he slipped his hands beneath the waistband of her jeans and pushed them down over her hips, stripping her completely in one fell swoop. He did not even leave her the flimsy barrier of her panties as protection.

This was the way he had wanted her all along, Judd realized with primitive exultation: open, vulnerable, needing him. With a sense of wonder and rising hunger he put out a hand to cover the dark, tangled thicket at the apex of her thighs. The feel of her was doing incredible things to him. It would be hard to make the passion last because his body was clamoring so loudly for satisfaction. But he wanted it to be good for her.

No, he thought savagely, he wanted it to be the best for her. So unbearably perfect that she would never again think of another man. He wanted to blot out any flickering dreams of romance and love she might be harboring in her feminine fantasies. He wanted to fill her thoughts solely with images of her surrender in his arms.

"Judd?" Her nails began to bite into the flesh of his shoulders and her legs curled and uncurled restlessly on the cot. When he looked up he saw that her eyes were tightly closed and in the moonlight he could read the strain of passion on her face.

"You want me, Honor, don't you? Tell me that you want me!"

"Oh, yes, Judd. So much." She gasped for breath as he began to explore the dampening heat between her thighs. "I never dreamed it could be this way!"

He stretched out beside her, tangling his legs with hers and finding an intense pleasure in the contrasting textures of their skin. She was so soft, so warm and inviting, Judd thought dazedly, how had he managed to keep his hands off her for the past three nights? Why hadn't he taken her that first night? Then he could have spent the rest of the time in Mexico in her arms. What a fool he'd been!

His hand shaped the curve of her thigh and she arched closer, turning her face into his shoulder. He felt the tiny shudder that coursed through her and gloried in the knowledge that his touch had elicited it.

Slowly, tantalizingly, he clenched his fingers into the resilient flesh of her buttocks.

"Ahhh!" he heard himself exclaim. "Honey, you feel so good. My God, I want you!"

When she responded by slowly trailing her palm down his chest until she found the flat, lean line of his stomach, Judd thought he would go out of his head. Deliberately he began to urge her legs apart by drawing small, erotic little circles on the outside of her thigh. She wriggled delightfully and he felt her toes, which were lying alongside his calf, begin to curl. The subtle sign of her passion inflamed him and he began to draw the circles much closer to the heart of her femininity.

Then her warm hand trailed shyly lower on his body, cautiously eager for the feel of him. He waited for an instant, aware that he was holding his breath in anticipation of her touch. When it didn't come he wrapped his arm around her back and pulled her closer, leaning over to whisper darkly, "Don't tease me tonight, lady. I can't take it. Put your hands on me and show me that you want me."

Then he thrust himself against her palm, sighing as she gently clasped the rigid manifestation of his desire. She leaned into his shoulder and sank her teeth lightly into the muscle there. Judd groaned heavily, his blood flowing like fire in his veins.

"Oh, my darling, Judd!"

Her soft words left him hungry for more of the same. He wanted to hear her call his name again and again in passion and he didn't think he would ever get enough of those small cries that came from far back in her throat. She was so exquisitely sensitive to his touch, he thought in pleased wonder, loving the way she moved every time he stroked her here or there or down the inside of her leg.

"Sweetheart, you're wonderful. Like fire in my arms." With his foot he drew her legs apart slowly. The deep surge of desire in his loins was an ache now that would have to be satisfied soon or he would go crazy. There could be no peace for him until he had taken Honor Knight completely.

"Darling Judd, I want you so!"

Her hands fluttered over him, driving him wild. He couldn't wait any longer. Dropping tiny, biting kisses along her shoulders and down her breasts Judd slowly eased himself over her until his shoulders blocked the path of moonlight to her face. In the shadows he could see the way she watched him from beneath passion-heavy lashes, her eyes deep with mystery and feminine desire.

In that moment she was woman, the primitive female whom he must take for his own. The urge to possess was on him in a way he had never known before, leaving him unable to contemplate any other ending to this night than total sensual victory.

He moved against her softness, seeking to bury himself in her warmth. She cried out as he took her completely, the impact of his body making itself felt on hers. For an instant he froze, fearful that he had hurt her, but when he scanned her face he realized she was too far lost in the realm of physical sensation to care, and then she was clinging to him.

"Honor, my God, *Honor!*" The feel of her nails on his back and of her legs surrounding him was incredibly intense. It was beyond anything he had experienced and it fed his desire as nothing else could have. She wanted him as badly as he wanted her. There was no aphrodisiac as potent as mutual hunger and need. Every fiber of his being responded to it.

He rode her body with the driving power that seemed to be flowing in him. Never had he felt so strong, so vibrantly alive or so shatteringly passionate. She called his name in short, breathless tones just the way he wanted to hear it. He felt her slender frame tighten and knew that he was going to be able to satisfy her fully. The knowledge thrilled him.

At the height of her response he saw the way her eyes squeezed shut and she clamped down on her lower lip with her own teeth. Then the tiny, delicate ripples of satisfaction began deep within her. He felt them at once and held himself in check so that he could enjoy her fulfillment before giving in to his own.

"Let go, sweetheart," he muttered. "Just let go. Let it take you, I'll keep you safe."

As if his insistent voice were all the urging she needed to send her over the edge, Honor shuddered in his arms and gave herself up to the finale of their passion.

"Judd, oh, please, Judd. . . ."

He could resist no longer. With a half-stifled shout of exultant satisfaction Judd followed her over the brink and into the drifting velvet beyond.

It was a long time before Honor came back to her senses. She floated blissfully for a while, luxuriating in the warm dampness of the male body against which she was curled. And then slow contentment curved her mouth and filled her sleepy eyes.

It had all been worth it. The risk of building the bridge of understanding on a foundation of passion had worked. She knew it had worked. There was no way a man and a woman could share what she had just shared with Judd and not wake up the next morning with an indestructible tie between them.

He had been as caught up in the rapture as she had been and he had shown her the tender, responsive side of his nature, the side he kept so well concealed most of the time. Judd Raven could not fool her any longer, she decided in wise, gentle, very feminine amusement. He was a man of passion and sensitivity. He had given all of himself, determined to satisfy her completely.

She had never felt so close to a man in her life. Who would have guessed that beneath that cold, controlled facade there was such elemental, sensual need? Yes, it had been a risk allowing him to sweep her off to bed like this, a risk she had feared from the beginning. But it had paid off in terms of commitment and under-standing.

For neither of them, she knew, could ever go back to where they had been before. Judd was no longer the hunter from the sky come to carry her off to destruction. He couldn't be. The two of them had just forged the most fundamental sort of bond. From this moment on Judd would be able to trust her. How could he unite them so completely and not be able to trust completely also?

For the first time in weeks a sense of welcome relief settled on Honor as she lay beside Judd. She had been facing the crisis so long and had been so alone that it seemed like a miracle to at last have an ally.

"What are you thinking, honey?" Judd asked soft-ly, stirring slightly beside her.

"Oh, Judd. I feel as if a great weight has been lifted from my shoulders. You can't imagine what a relief it is to feel so close to you now. I was so afraid of you."

His hand caught her shoulder and squeezed. "I don't want you to be afraid of me, sweetheart. Not ever."

"No." Her voice was lazy with contentment. "In the morning we can talk."

His grip on her shoulder tightened. "That's right, honey. We'll talk in the morning. We'll get everything straightened out."

Her fingers trailed lightly along his chest and she yawned daintily. "That first night . . ."

"Hmmm? What about that first night?" His voice sounded somewhat distant, as if he were sorting through his own private thoughts.

"I'm just wondering what it would have been like if you'd gone ahead and made love to me," she confessed.

"I've wondered the same thing," he murmured with a trace of amusement in his voice. "I've wondered like hell! But I couldn't have guessed it would be this good. Nothing's ever been this good for me, Honor."

She tried to resist but couldn't. The temptation was too much and she was feeling too lighthearted and close to him. "Not even kissing your airplane?"

That brought her a small, sharp slap on her naked rear end. "One of these days, Honor Knight, you're going to go too far with that lousy joke."

"I can't wait."

"You enjoy baiting me, don't you?" he asked, not sounding upset by the notion, merely interested.

"Sometimes. It's a way of getting a response from you. A human response."

"Now you know there's another way, don't you?"

She could sense that he was smiling and lifted her head to check. She saw him smile so rarely. He was.

Not a huge, laughing, masculine grin, just a small, upward tilt to his hard mouth, but it was there and it was real. And it was also in his eyes. That fact pleased her most of all.

"Yes," she agreed with rash pleasure. "Now I know there's another way."

"Good. Go to sleep, honey. We'll talk in the morning."

Trustingly she obeyed, curving her body close to his and relaxing into the promised security of his arms. In the morning everything would be all right.

"There's not much room on this cot, is there?" she noted, yawning again.

"We'll manage. Just don't wriggle too much."

"Yes, sir," she said with a chuckle and promptly fell asleep.

It wasn't the sun that woke her the next morning, it was the realization that someone was rustling around the tiny shack. Honor smiled to herself, opening her eyes slowly. Perhaps Judd was going to surprise her with breakfast. Had Paco already been by with the daily egg ration? She hadn't heard him knock.

In the dawn light she saw Judd across the room. He was packing his small overnight kit, not fixing breakfast.

"Judd? Why are you up so early? What are you doing?" She sat up slowly, frowning in bewilderment.

"I'm getting ready to leave, Honor. What do you think I'm doing? This is Saturday, remember?"

"So?"

"So this is the day I take you back to the man you claim isn't your father. This is the day you said you'd go with me in the Cessna without any more fuss.

Better get up, honey. It's getting late. I want to get off the ground as soon as possible."

Honor could only sit with the sheet clutched to her chin, staring at the stranger who had been her lover during the night. *He meant it.* He was still going to take her back to Garrison and Prager. She couldn't believe it.

A sick, panicky feeling welled up inside her. For a moment she thought she was going to faint. Where was the man who had become her ally and friend? Where was the man who had learned to trust her? With whom she had forged a sensual bond last night?

It was obvious that Judd Raven was still intent on being the unwitting instrument of her destruction. He trusted her no more this morning than he had yesterday.

Going to bed with him had changed nothing.

Chapter 6

JUDD SAW THE SUDDEN WHITENESS OF HER CHEEKS AND he started toward the bed, an uneasy feeling motivating him. He couldn't forget that scar on her wrist. Honor Knight appeared to be prone to the melodramatic and he didn't want any complications in his plans this morning.

"Honor!" he snapped sharply.

She looked up at him, hazel eyes huge with disbelief and pain. "Last night meant nothing at all to you, did it?" she whispered.

Was that all that was wrong? Judd almost smiled in relief. "Honey, last night was wonderful and you know it. I realize you probably want a little cuddling this morning, that's natural. But there just isn't time. I've got plans—"

"A little cuddling!" She looked utterly appalled. "I

don't want a little cuddling! I want a little trust! So last night was wonderful, was it? By that I take it you mean I was a good lay?"

"Honor." He frowned, uncertain about where all this was leading but knowing he was going to have to put a stop to it before it turned into some form of feminine hysteria.

"Well?" she dared, her eyes far too bright, her body drawn as taut as a bow string. "Well, Mr. Raven? Was I good? I mean, considering the fact that I am, after all, only a suicidal, runaway, neurotic female? Was last night worth the extra few days you spent here in Mexico?"

"Honor," he tried coldly, "don't turn hysterical on me. I don't have time for a lot of dramatics this morning."

"Too bad! Because I do have time for them! All the time in the world! I'm not going anywhere with you, damn it!"

"Honor, you said that if I gave you the extra time here in Mexico you'd go with me without a lot of trouble, remember?" he asked patiently.

"My life was at stake. I would have promised anything. But under the circumstances you'll have to forgive me for not being willing to live up to my promises." She scrambled off the cot, still clutching the sheet in front of her. He couldn't tell if that sheen in her eyes was from incipient tears or not, but he rather feared it was. "I will not get on that plane with you this morning! What's the matter with you, Judd? Are you really so inhuman that you can't trust anyone? Not even after what we shared last night?"

Judd looked at her across the cot. She was so

sweetly disheveled from the night, her hair in intriguing disarray. And she was quite naked behind that sheet. He could remember every inch of that nakedness. The memory of it warmed him even now when he had more crucial matters to deal with. Last night she had been infinitely soft and gentle and unbelievably passionate in his arms. What the hell was the matter with her this morning? She was staring at him as if he were a monster.

"I'm not, you know," he heard himself say.

"You're not what?" she nearly shrieked.

He winced at the edge in her voice. "I'm not a monster." He searched for the words he needed and realized he didn't know how to say what should be said. "Honor, last night was inevitable. Don't you know that? It became inevitable after that first night when you attacked me. I'd been wanting you since I began looking for you. After I found you I knew that sooner or later—"

"You knew that sooner or later you'd get me into bed and satisfy your curiosity about what it was like to lay a suicidal, compulsive liar, is that it? Now that you've satisfied your curiosity you're going to turn me over to Garrison and Prager, collect your two thousand and fly away into the wild blue yonder! You're disgusting. An arrogant, cold-blooded mercenary. I can't believe I was stupid enough to think that I could reach you on some human level. Last night—"

"You seem to have a slight misconception about last night," he interrupted icily. He felt an unaccustomed wave of anger at her accusations. Grimly he controlled it. Nothing was to be gained this morning by letting this little witch goad him into losing his temper. "You gave yourself to me last night, Honor. Do you really believe I'd casually turn you over to someone who wants to kill you?"

"That's exactly what you're planning to do!"

He shook his head, keeping his tone low and trying to sound soothing, which probably didn't work very well. He hadn't had much experience trying to soothe hysterical women. "You should be the one doing the trusting this morning, honey. You trusted me enough to surrender in my arms last night."

"I thought we were making love!" she hissed furiously. "It wasn't a case of my *surrendering*. I went to bed with you because I thought we could share something meaningful. I thought that afterward you'd realize I couldn't have been lying to you all along. I thought you'd know me intimately enough to trust me. My God, Judd, how can you be such a coldhearted bastard? Last night you seemed so . . . so *human!*"

Once again Judd had to clamp down firmly on the anger that threatened to erupt in response to her words. Why could this one woman out of all the people he had met make him come so close to losing his self-control over and over again? "I am human," he assured her, his voice more chilling than ever. "Enough of a man to want to protect what's mine. And make no mistake about it, Honor, you belong to me now. I'm going to take care of you. *Trust me!*"

"Trust you?" she gasped disbelievingly. "When you say you're going to hand me over to Garrison and Prager?"

"Will you just shut up and listen to me? I have a plan. . . ."

"What sort of plan?" she challenged.

"I'm going to get to the bottom of all this," he said

quickly, seeing an opening at last. "I'm going to find out exactly what's going on and I'm going to make sure you're safe during the process."

"What the hell is that supposed to mean?" she snapped, brushing her hand impatiently across her eyes. Damn it, she *was* crying.

"If you'll settle down and stop yelling at me I'll explain," he told her quietly. Instinctively he took a step toward the bed. The tears bothered him. But when she immediately backed away he stopped in annoyance.

"Don't touch me," she ordered shakily, putting out a hand to ward him off. "I don't want you touching me. Not after last night."

"Damn it to hell, woman! I don't know what you *think* happened last night, but I can tell you what actually *did* happen!" He ran his fingers restlessly through his hair and then planted his hands on his hips. It was either that or he was going to reach out and take hold of her. Something told Judd that that wouldn't be the wisest move at the moment.

"I *thought* we meant something to each other last night," Honor said tightly. "I thought that we would achieve some kind of understanding. I *thought* you'd realize that I wasn't lying to you. I *thought* we'd wake up this morning able to communicate with each other. I thought that making love together would give us a bond, a link that we could use to trust each other. I *thought* you'd listen to me this morning, that you'd *want* to listen to me. That you'd want to believe in me. That you couldn't do anything else!"

His eyes narrowed. "You wanted all that from one night in bed?" he asked in mild amusement.

"Don't you dare mock me! Yes, damn it, I did want

all that from one night in bed with you. I thought we were falling in love. Why the hell do you think I was willing to risk going to bed with you?"

A light began to dawn at the end of the tunnel and Judd realized what was happening. His expression softened and he shook his head ruefully. "Honey, you're a romantic, do you know that? You're trying to romanticize what was really a very straightforward, fundamental happening between two people. You're as attracted to me as I am to you. Last night you gave yourself to me and now you belong to me. It's as simple as that. Don't look for some rosy, mystical explanation for what was essentially something that wasn't rosy or mystical at all. It was something very basic. Don't romanticize last night, Honor. You'll just work yourself up into a state of hysteria and tears."

"And you don't need that this morning, do you?" she shot back scathingly. "You've got *plans!*"

"That's right," he agreed evenly.

"A cold-blooded mercenary," she repeated dully, sinking back down onto the cot with the sheet wrapped around her. She stared at the wall as if there were nothing left for her in life.

Judd started forward, aware of a violent desire to shake her until she stopped calling him names. Didn't she understand what had really happened last night? She was an intelligent female, even if she was prone to dramatics, even if she was more than a little prone to romanticizing situations. "Don't you want to hear my plans?" he charged.

She hesitated and then swung her wide, accusing gaze away from the blank wall to stare at him. "Go ahead," she ordered bitterly, "tell me all about how you're going to get me killed. But I would appreciate it if you wouldn't come any closer in the process. Just stay away from me."

"Damn it to hell! You're acting like a woman scorned this morning!"

"I am," she agreed, nodding once. "Very scorned."

He turned away from her because if he didn't Judd knew he would do something violent. With an effort of will he regained control of himself and went to stand on the far side of the small room. Leaning against the wall, his arms folded across his chest, he regarded her stubborn, proud profile.

"Honor, I'm going to make a phone call from the town where we'll be stopping for fuel. It's on this side of the border. I'm going to call the man you say is Leo Garrison and I'm going to tell him to meet me at the border with proof that he's really your father. We'll meet in front of all those U.S. border guards at one of the points of entry. There will be plenty of protection for you if he's not who he says he is."

She didn't move but he sensed she was at least listening. "I'll stay right beside you all the way until we get this whole thing sorted out," he went on encouragingly. "Even if he is your father, I won't abandon you to him. It's obvious there's something screwy about your relationship with him and I'm going to go along with you until I find out exactly what it is."

He watched her lashes lower briefly in despair but when she looked at him her gaze was clear and very level. There was no longer any sign of the budding hysteria. "And if he does show up with proof that I'm his daughter? Will you give me a chance to prove he's lying? Will you let me dig out my birth certificate? Will you protect me while I go to my safety-deposit box in Phoenix and find some proof of my side of the story? *Can* you protect me?"

"I can and I will," he vowed flatly.

She continued to watch him and for the first time since he had met her Judd realized he wasn't at all sure what she was thinking. It was strange to suddenly be confronted with that cool little mask. Up until now her emotional state had been easy to define. Her underlying vulnerability had been evident from the start and so had all her moods. Last night, for instance, there had been no doubt about the level of her response. But right at this moment he was at a loss to understand her state of mind. Judd's sense of unease grew. He didn't like the feeling that she was somehow managing to shut him out. Perhaps it was just his imagination. "Honor?" he finally prompted.

"I don't have much choice, do I?" she asked bluntly.

"No. Trust me, honey. That is the best way to handle this mess."

"Trust you," she echoed as if the words were in a foreign language. "Trust you?"

His eyes hardened but he didn't move away from the wall. "You told me once that you thought you could. You said that in my own way I was probably very trustworthy."

"But you don't trust me. Not even after last night," she whispered.

"Honor, be reasonable. Last night didn't prove a damn thing one way or the other. I'll tell you what last night was, it was a commitment. You gave yourself to me and now I'm going to take care of you."

"You sound as if we made some sort of bargain in bed!"

"I guess we did, in a way." He shrugged. "But I think the outcome would have been the same even if we hadn't gone to bed together. I've been realizing since that first night that there was something weird about this whole operation. I told you a couple of days ago I wouldn't turn you over to the guys who hired me until I found out for certain they really were your family."

She smiled then, a bitter, cold smile unlike any expression he had ever seen shape that mobile, vulnerable mouth. "In other words I would have been in exactly the same situation this morning whether or not I'd taken the risk of sleeping with you, is that it?"

Why did she have to talk about taking risks? There had been no risk in going to bed with him last night. Hadn't she known from the start that he would take care of her? "Honor, last night gave me the right to protect you. Don't you understand? Before that I was willing to stand by you as long as you felt you needed me but after last night I have the *right* to stand by you. There's a difference."

"Such logic," she gritted. Slowly she got to her feet and started toward the tiny alcove that served as a bathroom. The sheet trailed behind her. "All logic and no trust."

"Honor!" Perhaps he should take a firmer hand with her this morning, Judd decided uncertainly. She was such a temperamental, vulnerable little creature and she'd been under a lot of strain during the past month, regardless of the cause.

"Don't worry, Judd," she told him coolly from the doorway. "I'll go with you. I'll let you try your brilliant plan. But just in case it doesn't work and we both wind up with a bullet in the brain, allow me to tell you now that *I told you so!*"

Judd winced as the door slammed behind her. At least some of her natural fire was returning. For a few minutes there he'd thought she'd turned into a block of ice on him. And he hadn't liked it one bit.

Most of the village turned out to wish them goodbye and the children watched with wistful eyes as Judd went through a careful preflight check and then taxied out into the center of the dusty road.

Someday, he thought fleetingly as he taxied to the downwind end of the road and turned the Cessna into the wind, he'd like to give those kids a ride. He glanced at Honor's rigid profile as she sat stiffly beside him. "What do you think about maybe coming back sometime and giving everyone a ride?" he asked above the sound of the engine. "I can still remember my first plane ride. It changed my whole life," he added slowly.

"If you ask me it wasn't for the better," she muttered, refusing to look at him.

He sighed and concentrated on the tachometer once more before opening the throttle. She wasn't going to make life easy, but she wasn't actively fighting him. She might be furious, but at least she trusted him to some extent. Well, she'd get over her temper, Judd decided on a more positive note as he automatically corrected for the engine's torque and guided the Cessna down the makeshift runway. A moment later they were airborne as the reliable little plane climbed quickly and steadily into the blue Mexican sky.

"You know, you were damn lucky to get this far into rural Mexico without any major disasters," he remarked shortly after takeoff. "This part of the world is still pretty wild. There are still bandits in the hills and a woman traveling alone—"

"Might get herself kidnapped and killed?" she concluded laconically. "Well, what a coincidence. That's exactly what seems to be happening to me, isn't it? Except, of course, it wasn't the local people who turned out to be a threat."

After that, conversation lagged, to say the least. Judd freely acknowledged to himself that he didn't know a great deal about handling women. His relationships in the past had tended to be limited, superficial and fleeting in nature. He was well aware of the fact that he didn't have all that much to offer a woman. Females liked financial security, companionship and exciting romance. He'd never been able to provide any of the three. Women sometimes found him interesting, he knew, but they didn't tend to hang around long when it became obvious that he wasn't going to be able to provide the more basic components of a lasting relationship. Hell, he had a damn hard time even carrying on a long conversation with most women. It was different when Honor felt like talking to him, he thought. When she was in the right mood he found himself able to converse with her more than he'd ever been able to with anyone else.

Unfortunately she wasn't in the mood today. He wondered how long it would be before she was. When this mess was all sorted out it would be nice to take her away for a while, just the two of them. That thought buoyed his own mood until the time came to land for fuel and the all-important phone call to the States.

As was his practice Judd supervised the refueling of the Cessna personally. As far as he was concerned that sort of elementary precaution was on a par with a parachutist packing his own chute. Over the years he'd learned not to put his life in anyone's hands but his own. That sort of care had paid off more than once.

"There should be a restroom in the office over there," he told Honor as he paid for the fuel and took her arm. "You can use it while I make the phone call. It might take me a while to get a call through to the States. But this is a popular tourist area, so the local operators should be familiar with the procedure."

She didn't appear overly interested in the complexities of the Mexican telephone system. Judd shrugged, saw her into the restroom and went to find a phone. Fifteen minutes later he had the man who called himself Honor's father on the line. The courtly, charming manner was evident in the older man's tones, even through the faint static on the line. Hell, Judd thought idly, if the man was a phony he was an excellent actor.

"Mr. Knight? This is Raven. I've got your daughter with me."

"Oh, thank God, Mr. Raven. I can't tell you how relieved I am." He sounded it, too, Judd decided. "Where are you? Is Honor all right?"

"We're still in Mexico. A refueling stop. Honor is fine, but frankly she's not too thrilled at the idea of returning to the States."

"She's been giving you a sampling of her, uh, vivid

imagination, I take it?" The other man groaned
feelingly. "The poor girl. After all this time alone in
Mexico there's no telling how much ground has been
lost. Her therapist is so anxious to get her back under
his care."

"Well, to tell you the truth, I'm not sure she's going
to wind up back under his care," Judd informed his
employer sardonically. "She claims you're not her
father. Says you're a man named Leo Garrison for
whom she used to work."

"She is a very sick woman, Mr. Raven."

"Yeah, so you told me. She's going to make a scene
at the border when I have to land for customs, Mr.
Knight. I can predict it right now. I won't be able to
force her back into the plane if she throws herself on
the mercy of the officials. At the very least there's
going to be a major delay."

"Yes, yes I can see the problem. If her delusions are
stronger than ever . . ." Judd could practically hear
the older man thinking.

"I think the simplest way to handle this is to have
you meet us at the port of entry. You can take charge
of her there. Bring some proof that she's your daughter, though. The customs people might be a little
skeptical in a situation like this."

And then it came. With an adroitness that Judd
could only admire, the man identifying himself as Leo
Knight took the rope he had been offered and obligingly hung himself.

"I have a more practical idea, Mr. Raven. And one
that will mean a considerably larger fee for you. I'm
sure you can understand how anxious my family is to
avoid any embarrassment for Honor. This whole
escapade is going to be hard enough on her as it is, not

to mention on the rest of us. What would you say to simply flying her in over the border without stopping at a port of entry? I know that, strictly speaking, it's not legal, but you and I both know pilots slip back and forth over the border all the time without bothering with the formalities."

"Mostly when they're transporting something like cocaine," Judd agreed dryly.

"Which we aren't involved with at all!" There was a comradely laugh from the other end of the line. "I really do think this would be the easiest way to avoid a major scene at customs, don't you? I'll be quite happy to double your fee for the extra trouble."

"Where do you suggest we meet?" Judd asked quietly. It was his own fault, of course. He'd never given Knight/Garrison any reason to think he wouldn't do just about anything for the money. Still, after listening to Honor call him a mercenary for the past few days, Judd decided he was getting tired of other people assuming he could be bought. A man had to make a living, didn't he? Why the hell was he beginning to think he owed Honor an apology for the way he survived in this world?

"There's a small town just above Douglas, near the Arizona–New Mexico border . . ." The satisfaction in Garrison's cultured voice was blatant.

Judd listened attentively while he was given the name of the town, and then he slowly hung up the phone. The charges had been reversed but the call was going to cost Leo Garrison a lot more than money. When he turned around Judd found Honor standing a few feet away, her face strained. The green and gold of her eyes had never been more vivid as she awaited the verdict.

For an instant he just looked at her, knowing an incredible sense of relief. Then he stepped forward and gripped her shoulders. "It's okay, honey. Everything's okay. Knight or Garrison, or whatever his name is, just put his foot in it as far as I'm concerned. Don't worry. You're not going back to him."

Beneath his hands she seemed to crumple a little in her relief. He could feel the tension draining slowly from her slender frame. "Please," she murmured, "I'd like to sit down."

He led her anxiously over to one of the old wooden chairs that lined the ramshackle office and carefully eased her down. A new worry assailed him. "Are you all right, Honor? You're not getting sick, are you? You've been down here for quite a while and God knows the food and water aren't all that reliable."

"I'm fine." She sagged back in the chair, leaning her head against the wall. Her eyes were closed. "What did he say that convinced you he wasn't my father?"

Judd crouched down in front of her, taking one of her cold hands in his and chafing it lightly. What the devil was the matter with her? He'd told her all along he would take care of her. Was she actually faint with relief now that it was all over? Didn't she understand she'd had nothing to worry about?

"He tried to bribe me to take you in over the border without stopping at customs. As far as I'm concerned a worried father wouldn't have wanted to have his daughter exposed to that kind of risk. He would have met us at the border with his proof of identity and the doctor he seems to think you need so badly." Judd lifted one shoulder. "Maybe I'm just getting tired of being thought of as a complete mercenary. He didn't even bother trying to tell me he'd provide proof of his identity when we met at the rendezvous. He just assumed that for the right money I wouldn't ask too many questions."

She smiled bleakly. "So you've decided to trust me because he insulted you? Do I owe my life to the fact that you don't like being called a mercenary?"

He frowned. "No, it's just the logic of the situation. I've been trying to figure this mess out from the beginning. Your story was wild, Honor, you've got to admit. But Garrison's asking me to bring you in illegally over the border sure as hell doesn't sit right, either. Under the circumstances I'm not about to turn you over to the man."

"I see," she said quietly. "Thank you."

He blinked owlishly, not liking the cold formality of her voice. Well, she had been under a lot of strain lately. Judd got to his feet. "Come on, honey, let's get back in the air. We've got some flying to do."

"Where are we going now?" she asked, but she was getting obediently to her feet.

"Where you should have gone as soon as you realized you were in trouble: to the authorities. There's a man I know in Tucson. We're going to look him up and tell him your story. He can sort the rest of this out. He's good at things like that."

"But, Judd, I can't prove a thing! That's why I didn't go to the authorities in the first place!"

"We'll let Maddock worry about proving things. Let's go."

Two hours later they were in Tucson. With determined perseverance Judd pushed himself and Honor through several levels of red tape until Honor finally found herself talking to a harried-looking man in a rumpled suit and tomato-sauce-stained shirt. Judd never left her side as she wearily went through her tale over and over again. She was astounded when she was informed that the Feds were more than a little interested.

"Miss Knight, you are a godsend to a poor, struggling government employee," the man called Craig Maddock announced at the end of the long, trying interview. "We've had Garrison and Prager under investigation for months. We know they've been arranging shipments of arms out of this country and then selling them overseas, but there were too many missing facts for us to close the net. We didn't know about that San Diego warehouse, for example. We'll get in touch with the local people there and tell them to have a look."

"Mr. Maddock, I have no idea whether or not they're using that warehouse for anything illegal," Honor protested quickly. "I just happened to remember hearing Nick mention it one time." She had remembered a good many details under Maddock's persistent, skillful questioning. "I wondered why Garrison and Prager needed a warehouse but I never bothered to question it. I guess I just assumed it had something to do with a business sideline." Her voice trailed off weakly.

Judd leaned forward intently. He had been sitting beside Honor for the last two hours and he could see how utterly exhausted she was. "I think you've gotten just about everything out of her that you're going to get, Maddock. Let me take her someplace where she can get some rest. She's been on the run for weeks. She's had it."

Maddock nodded. "Should have come to us in the

first place," he told Honor firmly. "Could have saved yourself a lot of trouble."

"Yes, sir," she said politely, and only Judd recognized the underlying mockery. Good Lord! Couldn't she even resist baiting a government agent? But Maddock didn't appear to notice.

"With the information you've given us this afternoon we should be able to move quickly on the case. We *can* move quickly at times, you know," he added wryly. "Since this office has been handling the case from the beginning, we should be able to wrap things up fairly rapidly. Thanks to the rendezvous Judd has scheduled near the New Mexican border, we even know where Garrison and, perhaps, Prager will be this evening!"

"Come on, Honor," Judd ordered, helping her to her feet. "We're going to get a bite to eat and some rest." He glanced at Maddock. "You'll let us know when things are cleared up?"

Maddock nodded briefly, eyeing Judd coolly. "I'll let you know." There was a pause as Judd walked Honor to the door, and then Craig Maddock spoke again. "You came a little close to the line on this one, didn't you, Raven? One of these days you're going to find yourself stepping over the edge."

Judd went still for an instant, his hand on the doorknob. Then he threw a derisive glance back over his shoulder, his eyes meeting Maddock's in a level stare. When he spoke his voice was like silk. "Now, Maddock, you know I make it a policy not to ask too many embarrassing questions of my employers. Not when the money is good. Just think of all the little odd jobs I've done for you and your department over the years. And you never bothered to give me any more explanation beforehand than Garrison and Prager did!" He tugged Honor through the door and shut it firmly behind him. A mercenary. That was all he was even to people like Maddock, for whom he'd taken more than one risk. A damned mercenary.

It was over within twenty-four hours. Judd and Honor spent the night in an anonymous motel room near Interstate 10. No one except Maddock knew where they were. Judd fed a very quiet Honor dinner and then took her upstairs to the room. She was asleep before he got out of the shower. For several moments he stood watching her curled body under the bedclothes and acknowledged the depth of the strange possessiveness he was feeling.

Possessiveness was not a familiar emotion to him. What was it about this woman that had stirred it to life? She looked so tired, so vulnerable, lying there sound asleep. Very carefully, so as not to disturb her, he crawled into bed beside her. There was another double bed in the room but he had no intention of sleeping in it. Honor belonged to him now. He had saved her life.

Judd lay staring thoughtfully at the ceiling for a long time that night, thinking about where he would take his woman when this was all over. Perhaps Acapulco or one of the resorts in Baja. It was odd to plan a trip with someone else in mind. He had spent so many years alone with only himself to worry about that it felt distinctly strange to think in terms of taking care of someone else. Not bad, just odd. On that note he fell asleep.

It was the ringing of the telephone that awakened Honor the next morning. She came gradually alert, aware that she was not alone in the bed. Before she could figure out the location of the phone Judd had stretched an arm across her breasts with easy intimacy and picked up the receiver.

He lay propped on his elbow gazing down at her with dark, lazy eyes as he talked to Craig Maddock. Honor lay tense and uncertain, feeling trapped in the bedclothes. She hadn't meant to share the bed with Judd but she'd been so exhausted the previous evening that she couldn't even remember getting ready for bed. Obviously she hadn't been able to stay awake long enough to tell him he was to use the other bed, she realized in self-disgust.

"Okay, Maddock," Judd said finally. "I'll leave a number you can use to get in touch if you need us again. Okay. Yeah, sure, I understand. So long."

Honor tried to sink farther back into the depths of the bedding as Judd reached across her again to replace the receiver. He looked down at her, his dark gaze intent but not worried. "It's all over, honey. They picked Garrison up at the rendezvous point last night. He was armed. Prager is out of the country but they'll pick him up as soon as he sets foot back on U.S. soil. The Feds are going to keep Garrison's arrest quiet until they've got Prager, too. Maddock says they found several cases of illegal weapons in that San Diego warehouse, by the way. All the evidence they need."

"So it's really all over? Just like that?" she whispered, unable to believe that all the weeks of worry had finally ended.

Judd touched the side of her face with a strangely gentle finger. She stayed tensely still beneath his touch. "Everything's going to be okay now, honey.

I've been thinking. You're out of a job and I can afford to take a little time off even though I didn't get paid for bringing you out of Mexico. . . ."

Honor's expression must have warned him that he'd phrased that last part badly because Judd immediately shook his head, half-smiling. "I was only joking, honey. About getting paid, I mean. Anyhow, as I was saying, I thought we could go away together. Maybe Acapulco. Or there's a fancy resort on the tip of Baja. Would you like that? If you don't want to go back to Mexico, we could go to Hawaii. Whatever suits you," he ended magnanimously.

She tried to sit up in bed and he obligingly removed his hand so that she could do so. Without a word Honor pushed back the covers, her hands trembling with the force of her anger. Just who the hell did he think he was? The cotton nightgown she was wearing trailed behind her as she climbed out of bed and started toward the bathroom. She had only one goal in mind now: to get dressed and go home.

"Honor?"

The white sheet fell to Judd's bare waist as he sat up, frowning. Honor glanced back and saw the faint uncertainty in his face and wondered at it. Did he really think she'd go anywhere at all with him now? What blind arrogance!

"Go wherever you like, Judd. Have fun." She padded across the floor toward the bathroom and turned once more to cast him a chilled look. "Don't worry, you won't come out of this job unpaid. I'll be happy to give you the two thousand I owe you. I wouldn't want you to think I'm going to stiff you out of your normal fee!"

The lines of his face hardened into that familiar

unemotional mask. Honor saw the promise of menace there but she chose to ignore it. She was safe now. She had nothing to fear. "What the hell are you saying, Honor?" he bit out.

She pretended to consider the question. "I suppose I'm feeling reasonably grateful now that it's all over. I know I should thank you for getting me out of that situation, even though you did it in your own unique fashion. Lucky for me you do have a few scruples, isn't it? But you'd probably rather have the two thousand than my thanks, anyway."

"Damn it, Honor!" He started to climb out of the bed behind her. "What is it with you today? Are you still worn out? Do you need more rest?" He glared at her, clearly trying to work out an explanation for her cool behavior. It was obviously not what he had been expecting.

"I'm fine, Judd." She managed a very brilliant smile. "Now, if you will excuse me I'm going to take a shower and then I'm going to pack and go home to Phoenix. I hope you'll have a good time all alone on your vacation. You probably will. You seem quite accustomed to spending time by yourself."

His expression was set in the savage lines of a bird of prey. "You're coming with me, Honor," he stated evenly. "To Acapulco or Hawaii. You belong to me now. We're going to get to know each other, be together. Live together!"

"That's not possible, Judd."

"What the hell do you mean, it's not possible?" he demanded.

Honor took a deep breath and then said what had to be said. "Judd, I'm grateful to you for ending the crisis. But I can never forget that when the chips were down you didn't really trust me. That night we spent together was not the turning point for you that it was for me. I gave you everything I had to give that night and the next morning you just went ahead with business as usual." She moved one hand in a flat gesture of finality. "Whatever I was beginning to feel for you down in Mexico died the morning after we made love. You killed it when you made it plain that the night we had together meant nothing to you in terms of trust or love or anything else that's important."

"For God's sake, Honor! I saved your life! I rescued you! How the hell can you stand there and tell me you feel nothing for me now?"

"I didn't say I felt nothing. I said I was grateful, remember?" she reminded him harshly. "But that's all I feel. I'm damn grateful Garrison was dumb enough to give himself away on the phone and I'm grateful you had enough in the way of scruples to bother checking out my story. But I'm not going to sleep with you out of gratitude! The man I choose to sleep with will be someone who loves and trusts me completely. A man who would go to the wall for me just because he cared. He wouldn't demand proof of my innocence. He wouldn't wait to work out the *logic* of the situation before he decided which side to take. He'd be on my side come hell or high water, regardless of the damned logic of the thing!" She was aware that her voice was rising and her hands were clenching into fists. Deliberately Honor took deep breaths, striving to regain her control. She had lost her self-control far too many times with this man. It was time she took a leaf out of his book!

"Honor, I made it clear I would protect you right

from the start!" Judd raked a hand through his hair, dark eyes gleaming with frustrated anger. "What more did you want from me?"

"Trust. I wanted you to be one hundred percent on my side, no questions asked. I wanted you to have absolutely no doubts about me."

"Just because we'd been to bed together?" he demanded incredulously.

"Because I thought we'd made love together," she corrected savagely. "But I was wrong, wasn't I? Nothing changed for you that night. You woke up the next morning still the same cold, unemotional robot you were before you went to bed with me. Well, you got your proof and you did your duty by rescuing me. But don't expect anything more than gratitude from me, Judd Raven. Because I haven't anything more to give a cold-blooded mercenary who trusts his damned airplane more than he does me!"

She walked into the bathroom and shut the door far too quietly behind her.

Chapter 7

THE APARTMENT IN PHOENIX HAD NEVER LOOKED MORE inviting. Honor turned the key in the lock, knowing a vast sense of relief at being home. There had been too many lonely nights of wondering if she would ever be able to return. Her rakish little Audi was still parked sedately in the drive where she had left it that morning so long ago. Honor wondered if the battery still functioned.

The inside of the spacious one-bedroom apartment was exactly as she had left it, except, she noted wryly, all her plants had died. No, the little collection of exotic cacti in the corner by the window appeared to have survived. She walked across the white carpet to examine the array of thorny plants.

Other than the dead house plants, everything looked fine, in fact. It was hard to believe that nothing in her home had changed, when she herself had been

through so much. The sophisticated yet softly romantic decor looked as it always had. The meandering
peach velvet sofa, which formed an S shape in front of
the white fireplace, didn't even look dusty. The gilt
antique desk in front of the garden window was still
piled high with the books and papers she had left on
it. There was even a delicate bone china coffee cup
left on the round oak dining table.

She was home.

With a sigh of relief Honor carted her small suitcase
into the bedroom, slinging it onto the round, flounced
bed. She was home, but for a while there in Tucson
she hadn't been at all sure she was going to be able to
make the last leg of her journey. The raven who had
hunted her down in Mexico didn't appear inclined to
relinquish its prey.

There was nothing Judd could actually have done to
stop her from going home, Honor told herself briskly
as she unpacked, but all the same she had known
more than a shade of uncertainty when she'd faced
the implacable expression in those night-dark eyes.

Still, by refusing to succumb to the uneasy fear he
generated in her, she had made it out of the motel
room that morning and into a cab. From there she had
gone to the airport and hopped one of the short flights
to Phoenix. Honor hadn't dared to glance back as the
cab pulled away from the motel, but she had sensed
Judd watching her from the window.

There had been no mistaking his mood, either, she
reminded herself grimly. Every line of his lean, hard
body had been almost vibrating with the effort of will
he was exerting to hold himself in check. Honor had
been unable to escape from the dangerous confines of
the motel room quickly enough as far as she was

concerned. At any moment she had feared Judd would simply stop fighting his instincts, reach out and grab her. She still wasn't certain how he had managed to control himself. Maybe it was simply that he'd spent so many emotionless, self-controlled years already that he wasn't sure how to let go, even in anger and frustration.

Whatever it was that had held him in check during those tense moments while she changed into her jeans, called a cab and fled the room, Honor decided she was safe now. Judd might have decided he wanted her, but she was sure he would recover from the fleeting emotion as soon as she was out of the picture.

He could damn well go back to his airplane for all she cared!

Judd Raven seemed to have the emotional responses of a wild creature, a lone hunter who had spent far too much time by himself. He could be provoked to lust or to violence but he didn't waste emotional energy on more refined feelings like trust and love.

Honor dashed a hand across her eyes as she piled her clothes into the washing machine. Now why in hell was she crying? It was because her own emotional reactions weren't nearly so limited as Judd Raven's, she assured herself. She had been through a trying ordeal and it was natural for her body to work off some of the stress. She was willing to bet Judd had never cried a tear in his life!

Morosely she stood staring at the glass door of the washing machine, watching as the clothes sloshed around. For some reason the scene that day by the village stream flashed into her mind and she remembered Judd's expression as he'd finally figured out that she was playing a game with him, a game he could

win. For just a short while, there had been traces of
genuine laughter in those glittering dark eyes. And
she, idiot that she was, had assumed from such limited
evidence that the man was human and that he could
be reached on a human level.

Honor turned away from the sight of the spinning
clothes. The last thing she wanted to recall was her
own weak, very human and all too female nature!
How could she have been so emotionally stupid as to
read so much into that single night in his arms? She
had actually awakened the next morning believing
herself to be falling in love with the man!

And all he'd felt was male satisfaction at having
conquered a woman to whom he'd been attracted.

Honor didn't lie to herself now. She knew Judd was
right when he accused her of romanticizing what was
merely a straightforward physical relationship. Well,
she'd learned her lesson. What in hell had made him
think she'd stick around for more of the same? In
rising disgust Honor realized she was having to dash
away more dampness from her eyes.

The business of settling back into her normal round
of activities began within twenty-four hours of her
return to Phoenix. Honor threw herself into the task
with a vengeance, knowing she needed outside stimuli
to help her recover both emotionally and physically
from the weeks of feeling hunted.

There were a lot of complicated explanations to
make, too, she soon discovered. Her unannounced
departure to Mexico had taken all her friends by
surprise. Many had assumed she was still in Hong
Kong. No one knew she'd been south of the border.

Not wanting to go into a long, involved explanation

of her absence, Honor brushed off the questions by saying she'd wanted some time away after her return from the Orient. Steve Melbourne, however, demanded a bit more in the way of explanations.

"So you're finally back from Hong Kong?" her former boyfriend began without preamble when she phoned him the morning after her return. "Sylvia told me you were back in town. And without that guy Prager, too. Can I hope for the best? Are you free tonight, for example?"

Honor took a deep breath and then smiled to herself. "Oh, yes, I'm quite free tonight, Steve." She had never felt so free in her life!

"And Prager?"

"I'm not seeing him anymore," she murmured feelingly.

"Great! Pick you up at seven. We can toast each other's freedom."

"What's that supposed to mean? You're not seeing Evie these days?"

"She took that job in Denver. I guess she's made her priorities pretty clear, hasn't she?"

"Steve, you know she would have been a fool to turn down that promotion," Honor chided gently.

"What about me? What the hell was I supposed to do? Give up my job and follow her to Denver?"

"One of you had to do something or give up the relationship. I gather you've chosen to abandon the relationship."

"I'll tell you all about it tonight. I could use a nice shoulder to cry on."

Steve Melbourne wasn't crying when he arrived at seven o'clock that evening, but it was obvious he'd been under something of a strain. They had developed an easy friendship since the end of their romance, and Honor sympathized with him, although she had felt powerless all along to help the situation between him and Evie Newcomb.

"It's this damned women's lib business," Steve complained over drinks in a pleasant fireside lounge. His light blue eyes were meditative and somewhat resentful. Steve was a good-looking man in his early thirties, a very corporate-looking man, Honor had often thought. The kind you couldn't imagine in anything besides a three-piece suit, even here in Phoenix where people tended toward the casual. His tawny hair and tanned features fit well with the business image. He was also very good at his job of comptroller for a large Phoenix firm. He'd go far, but so would Evie Newcomb. It looked as if they weren't going to make the journey together.

"Come on, now, Steve, one of the things you've always admired about Evie was her brilliance on the job. It was natural she'd be faced with this kind of decision sooner or later. You must have seen it coming."

"Yeah, I suppose so. I was living in a fantasy world thinking we could have it all. You can't have it all these days, can you, Honor? Maybe you never could."

"You can still make your own choices," she reminded him.

"You mean follow her to Denver?"

"You could get a good job there. It probably wouldn't hurt you at all careerwise," Honor pointed out gently.

"If she loved me she would have stayed here in Phoenix!"

"If you loved her you'd go to Denver."

Steve shrugged uneasily. "Looks like a no-win situation. But I really didn't bring you out tonight to spend the whole evening talking about me and Evie. Tell me what you've been doing for the past few weeks. No one knew when you were coming back. No one was even sure where you were. We just assumed you'd stayed in Hong Kong for some extra sightseeing."

"I, uh, had some time, so I did a little traveling," she told him dryly. For some reason she simply didn't feel like going into all the details. Not yet. Her reticence seemed to make him all the more curious, however, and she found herself deliberately looking for ways to switch the topic of conversation.

"Is it Prager? Are you upset about not seeing him anymore?" Steve finally asked commiseratingly.

"To tell you the truth, I hope I never see that man again!" Honor saw the astonishment on her friend's face and laughed ruefully. "I'm not working for Garrison and Prager anymore, Steve. As a matter of fact, I shall be pounding the pavement soon, looking for a job. Any ideas?"

"Sure. How about Evie's old job?" he shot back wryly.

"Oh, she'd love to hear that I was working in the same firm as you! I think she was always a little jealous that I knew you first."

"Maybe it would bring her back to Phoenix," he hazarded wistfully. "You know, there was something to be said for the good old days when a man could just pick out a woman, hunt her down and drag her back to his cave and keep her there."

Honor blinked, aware of a chill down her spine. A

man like Steve would never step out of his three-piece suit long enough to resort to such primitive methods. Steve Melbourne was well and truly trapped in the bonds of twentieth-century civilization. He, like most of the other men of his era, were learning to deal with women within the framework of the new social mores.

Looking at her friend across the small candle in the center of the table Honor suddenly realized just how different Steve Melbourne and the other men of her acquaintance were from Judd Raven. It made her realize just how lucky she had been to walk out of that motel room alone the previous morning. Raven's hunting instincts were definitely pre–twentieth century, as was his lack of refined sensitivity. She shivered in the warm, smoky lounge and remembered the rustic cantina where she had first seen Judd.

In all honesty, she admitted now, Judd's instincts, primitive as they were, had been correct on one score. He had been right when he'd said she couldn't have ever been truly involved with Steve Melbourne in a full-scale love affair. She knew in her heart that if she'd ever felt a fraction of the passion with Steve that she'd experienced with Judd, there would have been no way she could sit across from Melbourne tonight and be a "friend."

"Hey, don't go moody on me," Steve complained good-naturedly. "Come on, let's dance. I haven't danced since Evie left town."

Honor managed a smile, setting down her drink. "What are friends for?"

There was a certain solace to be had in dancing with a friend, however, Honor discovered. She still had so many disturbing memories that had to be banished. Neither she nor Steve would be making any demands on each other tonight and she knew she could relax and give herself up to the pleasures of simple friendship.

Friendship. That was another of the refined sides of human nature about which she doubted Judd Raven knew very much. He seemed singularly lacking in friends from what little she had learned about him. Even his association with Craig Maddock, for whom he had apparently worked from time to time, seemed more of a wary, adversary relationship than a friendship.

That faint flicker of unease coursed through her once more and she found herself clinging a little closer to Steve Melbourne than she might ordinarily have done. What was the matter with her? She was safe.

"Will you be looking for a position similar to the one you're leaving at Garrison and Prager's firm? A sort of administrative assistant post?" Steve asked musingly.

"Yes, I imagine so. That seems to be the kind of work I do best: coordinating schedules, lining up details, summarizing data."

"Evie always said you were very good at the administrative end of business and good with clients, too. That should be a marketable combination."

"I hope so."

"Might be tough to find another job that involves all that great overseas travel, though," Steve went on.

"Believe me, I've had my fill of travel for a while!"

"I wish Evie hadn't been so interested in traveling to Denver." He sighed.

"Steve, you're going to have to make a choice. How much does Evie mean to you?" Honor asked firmly.

"A lot," he groaned. "A hell of a lot."

Honor was genuinely glad to hear he had found with Evie the passion that had been missing in her own romance with him.

"Then what are you going to do about the situation?"

He looked down at her bleakly. "You're saying I should start job hunting in Denver?"

"It's up to you, but it would definitely be one way of showing Evie how much you cared, wouldn't it?"

"It would be a risk. . . ."

"Women have been taking that kind of risk for men for years!"

He smiled wryly. "You've got a point. I never thought of it that way before. I like to think I'm a modern sort of man, but sometimes I think life would be simpler if I weren't quite so modern."

"Evie probably wouldn't be half so interesting to you if *she* weren't so modern!"

"Ouch!" Steve chuckled ruefully. "I'm afraid you're right."

It wasn't until the music drew to a close that Honor saw Judd.

For an instant, as she came off the floor on Steve's arm, Honor was transported back to that night in the smoky cantina when she'd first seen her hunter. Everything stood still as she absorbed the impact and the implications of his presence.

He was sitting in a darkened booth at the back of the room. Dressed in black he seemed a part of the shadows around him. But the glittering dark eyes burned with a cold, intense fire that seemed to reach out to trap her. He didn't move as she stumbled slightly at Steve's side, simply sat quietly watching her as if she were prey that he could take his time collecting. There was no place she could run.

"Honor? Are you all right?" Steve's concerned tones brought her head around a little too sharply.

"Yes. Yes, I'm fine. I just need to sit down for a while. Too many drinks on an empty stomach, I suppose." What was Judd going to do? Would he cause a scene there in the lounge? Would he bide his time and follow her home? Would he wait for her in the parking lot? Intense panic gripped her.

Because there could be no doubt about why he was there. No amount of rationalization would explain his presence. Judd had followed her to Phoenix and she knew from the quiet, intent way he watched her that he was on the hunt once again. And once again she was to be the prey.

Belatedly her survival instincts began to assert themselves. Damn him to hell! She was not a silly, panicked little creature to be stricken helpless by the mere approach of the hunter. She could run, she could fight back, she could summon help. This wasn't Mexico and she wasn't alone and friendless. Judd Raven would not find her such an easy victim this time!

"Honor? Are you sure you're all right? Why don't I order us some appetizers?" Steve's voice grew more concerned as he carefully seated her.

She looked at him rather blankly, unable to focus on him because every fiber of her being was too vividly aware of Judd on the other side of the lounge. "That . . . that would be great, Steve."

"You stay here and I'll go find the hostess. If we

wait for her to come around to us in this crowd we'll starve to death!"

"Oh, no, please! You don't have to go find her . . ." But he was already on his way, weaving through the crowded lounge in search of the cocktail waitress. Honor felt abandoned and trapped. She sat frozen, not daring to glance in Judd's direction. Would he approach her now that Steve had left? This wasn't Mexico. He couldn't just drag her out of here, she reassured herself. Then she tried another swallow of her drink, seeking courage.

For five long minutes she sat, refusing to let her gaze be drawn to the corner where Judd was seated. They had to be the longest five minutes of her life. At any moment she expected to feel herself seized in the raven's talons and carried away. Dressed in a soft crepe off-the-shoulder dress of chrome-yellow she felt very vulnerable. A wide purple band emphasized her slender waist and the bright color combination made her feel suddenly very conspicuous. She would have given anything if she'd only decided on a darker, less vibrant dress that evening. How could you hide in the shadows when you were wearing something this exotic?

Damn it! Why did she feel she had to hide? She tried another sip of liquid courage and told herself there was nothing Judd could do to her as long as she stayed close to Steve.

Which brought up the rather dismaying question of what Judd did intend to do to her. He hadn't been pleased yesterday morning when she'd walked out of that motel room, but he'd made no real move to stop her. Not then. He'd been firmly under control, as usual. What had made him decide to come after her? Perhaps birds of prey simply didn't like the idea of having their victims walk away without permission.

Was that it? Was he there for vengeance? Was that another of the rather primitive emotions Judd had in his limited repertoire? Possessiveness? God! She was going to drive herself crazy wondering what he was thinking and when he would pounce. Her fingers trembled around the glass in her hand, and, unable to resist any longer, she cast a quick, furtive glance toward him.

He hadn't moved. But he was still watching her with that gleaming, utterly ruthless expression. When their eyes met he raised his glass in a small salute but made no move to get up and approach her.

Anger blazed in her as she allowed herself to stare at him. Who the hell did he think he was to intimidate her this way? She was not going to sit there and wait for him to come and get her. A slow fury began to replace the nervous dread she had been experiencing and she snatched her eyes away from his emotionless expression to glance around for Steve.

Melbourne was at the bar gathering up a tray of peanuts and a couple of drinks. He saw her look at him and smiled, starting back through the crowd toward her.

When he reached the table she leaned forward impulsively, her fingers touching his jacket sleeve. "Steve, I'm awfully sorry, but would you excuse me for a moment, please? Someone I know is sitting on the other side of the room and I really should run over and say hello."

"Well, sure." Steve glanced around questioningly but didn't seem to spot Judd. "I'll be glad to come with you. Or feel free to invite whoever it is over for a drink with us. . . ."

"That's all right. This won't take but a minute. I'll be right back."

Resolutely Honor got to her feet, automatically picking up her small clutch, and turned to make her way toward Judd's table. In that moment she couldn't have said where she got the nerve to make the first move. It was not normally in the nature of the quarry to confront the hunter. But it seemed to Honor that she'd been doing far too much running lately.

From across the room he sat watching as she moved toward him. His glittering jet eyes never left her face. Honor felt as if she were walking toward disaster but she refused to turn and flee from it now. She could tell nothing by the expression on his face. His features were set in harshly carved lines that betrayed nothing of his inner thoughts. Or perhaps that wasn't quite fair, she told herself wryly. Perhaps that mask of his was the perfect expression of his personality: hard, cold, implacable, emotionless.

A foot away from his table she stopped, calling on all her inner strength to handle the coming scene. "Good evening, Judd. What a coincidence seeing you here tonight. Going to be in town long?" Her voice was too light, too brittle, but it was under control.

"No."

"Another of your famous monosyllabic answers? A man of few words, aren't you, Judd?" She didn't want to acknowledge the way even a single word from him stirred her nerves. Honor kept her head high and her eyes as cold as possible.

"Is your friend a better conversationalist?" Judd asked far too politely.

"Infinitely!"

"Were you planning on going home with him tonight?"

"Yes!" she lied passionately.

"Have you told him about me?"

"No!"

"You're starting to talk in monosyllables yourself," Judd pointed out mildly.

"Judd, what are you doing here?"

"Watching you flirt with that guy in the three-piece suit."

"Are you drunk?" she challenged suddenly, eyeing his glass.

"Straight tonic water. Tastes awful." He took another sip.

"Well, that's a switch from the tequila, I suppose," she muttered nastily.

He shrugged. "I never drink before flying."

"You're planning on flying tonight?" she asked, feeling the first slight flickerings of relief. "You're going to leave Phoenix this evening?"

"Yes."

"Then you *are* just here on business?" She didn't quite believe that, but in that moment she wanted to believe it.

"In a manner of speaking."

"Judd—"

"Shall we go, Honor? It's getting late and we've got a long flight ahead of us." Judd set down the glass with an air of finality.

Honor sucked in her breath and automatically fell back a step as he raised his unreadable dark eyes to hers. Except that they weren't entirely unreadable now, she realized in shock. She had thought as she'd crossed the room toward him that his expression was the same emotionless mask she had first seen in Mexico. When he'd spoken to her there had been that familiar, cool tone in his words. But quite abruptly she realized that there was something new and brilliantly dangerous in his dark gaze.

Judd Raven was barely in control of himself tonight. A dark, savage flame of fury burned in him and she was the focus of it.

Honor backed away another step, other small bits of evidence forcing themselves on her attention. She saw the way his knuckles were almost white as he gripped the glass of tonic water. The brackets at the edges of his mouth were taut lines of menace. There was an unfamiliar rigidity in his lean, coordinated frame, as if the force of his anger were an electrical charge.

Desperately she licked her lips, trying to regain her composure. "Don't be ridiculous, Judd. I'm not going anywhere with you. This isn't Mexico. I don't have to go anywhere with you again!"

"You're coming with me tonight, Honor."

"No! Never!"

"If you involve your friend in the three-piece suit I'll probably wind up having to hurt him badly. Think about that when you go back to his table."

"You can't do this and you know it!" she hissed.

"Watch me."

"Judd! Stop this! You know damn good and well you can't threaten me now."

"I'm not threatening you. I'm here to collect what's mine. Very simple."

"I don't belong to you," she breathed.

"I saved your life."

"That doesn't give you any right! And besides, I didn't particularly approve of the way you went about it, remember?" she grated fiercely.

"You didn't understand at the time. I'm going to try and make everything very clear to you this time around. Are you coming with me now or is it going to be like it was in Mexico? Are we going to have to do it the hard way?"

She gasped. "You arrogant bastard! Go to hell, Judd Raven! I'm not going anywhere with you ever again!" Spinning around on her heel Honor fled back through the crowd to where Steve Melbourne waited.

"Honor? Are you okay? You look upset. . . ." Steve climbed to his feet, an anxious expression on his handsome features.

"Take me home, please, Steve. I've just had a very upsetting conversation with my acquaintance. I really would like to go home."

"Well, sure, if that's what you want. Should I say something to your friend? He had no right to upset you like this." Steve frowned, collecting Honor's purple shawl and taking her arm to guide her toward the door.

"No, no, it's nothing." Belatedly she remembered Judd's warning. "It was just some news about a mutual friend of ours that upset me." She mustn't involve Steve. She didn't want to bear the guilt for putting him in Judd's path.

She didn't dare glance in Judd's direction as Steve escorted her out of the lounge but she could feel the eyes of the raven on her as she walked out the door. Where could she go? A wave of hysteria welled up inside her as Steve drove her back to her apartment.

That was the same question she'd asked herself the night she had fled Hong Kong. Which way lay safety?

Over and over again she tried to tell herself that this time there was no need to run, but no amount of rationalization could make her forget the dark fury burning in Judd's eyes that night.

She'd seen him frustrated, even annoyed and angry, but never had she seen this kind of blazing rage. He was the hunter who'd had his prey snatched from his grasp. Nothing would satisfy him but to regain possession of it.

Perhaps she could contact Craig Maddock? Did the government man have any real control over Raven? Honor wasn't at all sure that he did. Judd was a law unto himself. Maddock had implied as much when he'd warned Judd that he was coming close to the edge. Surely terrorizing her was taking a step over the line? But what could Maddock do about it? What could anyone do about Judd Raven once he'd decided on his target?

"Good night, Steve," she said as the car drew up in front of her building. "I'm really sorry to have to end the evening so abruptly. Perhaps some other time?"

"I'll walk you to the door," Steve began, only to have Honor wave him aside.

"No, that's fine. I've got my key ready. Don't worry about hanging around. Please. I'll see you soon. Good night," she said again and practically leaped from the car.

Steve Melbourne's car pulled reluctantly back out into the street just as she turned the key in her lock, and Honor was both relieved and appalled to see him leave. He didn't really represent protection, she reminded herself. He would only get hurt if he got in Judd's way and she didn't want to be responsible for that.

Hurriedly she let herself inside the dark apartment, flipping on the light switch with impatient fingers and glancing around. A part of her had been half-afraid that she would not find herself alone, but she was safe. There was no raven waiting to pounce from the shadows. How much time did she have? Five minutes? Ten? Would Judd follow her straight from the lounge or would he take his time? He'd seemed in no hurry.

It went against the grain, against every bit of pride she possessed, but Honor knew that she was going to run again. She needed to get out of Judd's reach and the only way to do that was to flee. Surely his fury would wear itself out. He couldn't be feeling anything more for her than frustrated desire. He didn't have any more meaningful emotions, she told herself savagely. But how strong was his desire? How far would he follow her to assuage it?

She threw her clothes into the suitcase, not bothering to fold anything. Jeans, shirts, underwear, a toothbrush. God, she was getting good at this. Too good. In a matter of minutes she knew she had the essentials. Then she grabbed her purse, which still contained the money she'd brought back with her from Mexico.

California. This time it would be California. A big city like L.A. where even a raven would find the hunting tough. Then she'd call Maddock and ask for help.

Picking up the car keys on the way down the hall, Honor opened the front door and stepped out onto the walk, her suitcase in her hand. She only took one step before she realized that this time there would be no chance to run.

Judd stepped out of the shadows at the end of the walk, striding toward her with the relentlessness of a circling bird of prey.

She was trapped.

Chapter 8

HIS VOICE WAS STILL EVEN, BUT HIS WORDS TERRIFIED her. "You can't run and hide from me, Honor. I'm the man who can find you in the heart of Mexico. I found you here in Phoenix. And I'd have found you regardless of where you decided to run tonight."

"Damn you, Judd! You have no right to terrorize me like this! I'll call Maddock! I'll call the police, I swear it. Leave me alone. You've done all the damage you're going to do in my life!"

"What about the damage you've done to mine?" he startled her by asking. He was only a couple of feet away. In another moment he would be able to put out his hand and touch her. Honor stepped back into the doorway.

"What on earth are you talking about?" she breathed, her eyes widening.

"Never mind," he muttered abruptly. "We can talk

this all out later. Right now I'm in a hurry. Have you got everything you'll need?" He came to a halt in front of her and gestured at the suitcase in her hand.

"Need for what?" She glared at him warily.

"For a vacation in New Mexico, naturally," he drawled. "That's where we're going this evening."

"Not on your life!" She jumped backward and tried to slam the door. It caught on the immovable object of his booted foot. "Judd, I mean it! You can't do this! Not in this country!"

"This is between you and me," he grated. "It's got nothing at all to do with the laws of the nation." He thrust open the door and reached for her.

Honor dropped the suitcase and turned to flee. It was a useless exercise. Without any apparent effort Judd caught her lightly around the waist, pulling her back against him. When she tried to strike out at him with her hands he snagged her wrists. Holding her as she panted and struggled in the circle of his arm, he withdrew a length of fabric from one pocket.

"Judd, don't you dare!" Honor choked, outraged. But he ignored her, binding her wrists with a few deft twists of the fabric strip. She opened her mouth to scream and found herself gasping for breath as he heaved her easily over one shoulder.

By the time she recovered enough to attempt another shout for assistance Judd was picking up her suitcase and locking the front door. Then he was striding back down the walk toward a dark car parked at the curb.

"This is kidnapping!" she charged furiously as he stuffed her not ungently into the front seat of the car and slid in beside her.

He started the engine, not glancing at her as he

pulled away from the curb. "I see it more as a matter of recovering temporarily strayed property. Who was he, Honor? And if you make a try for that door I'll stop the car and tie your feet, too."

She slanted a baleful glance at him but withdrew her questing fingers from the door handle. The car was moving too swiftly now, anyway. She'd probably be killed if she tried to jump. Her outrage and anger simmered at a high level but she certainly wasn't feeling suicidal. There was another factor involved here, too. Now that he'd actually put his hands on her again she realized she wasn't genuinely afraid of him. Incensed, furious, angry, all of those, but not precisely afraid. He hadn't hurt her when he'd caught her and bound her hands. In fact, when she considered that he had been in a cold rage when she'd first seen him this evening, his touch had been surprisingly gentle. But, then, never in the time she had known him had Judd Raven actually hurt her physically.

"Honor?" he prompted darkly.

"He was a friend." She was aware they were on the Interstate and wondered briefly at their destination. The airport?

"That Melbourne guy you told me about?"

"Yes! A friend! Do you know what a friend is, Judd? It's someone you can talk to. Someone you can share your troubles with. Someone who understands you. Someone who wants to help you when you're in trouble."

"You didn't go to him for help when you got in trouble with Garrison and Prager," Judd pointed out flatly. "You ran all by yourself to Mexico."

"I didn't want to expose him to any danger."

"Because you knew he couldn't handle it?"

"For heaven's sake, Judd! What's the point of all this questioning?" she gritted, sinking into her corner and staring morosely out the window at the passing lights of the city.

"If we had been *friends* before you found yourself in that mess with Garrison and Prager, would you have come to me for help?" he persisted coolly.

She shot him an uncertain glance. What was he getting at? "Talk about an academic question! What on earth makes you ask that?"

"Just curious. Would you have asked me for help, Honor?"

He was deadly serious, she realized. Sighing, she gave up the attempt to avoid the question. "Maybe," she admitted cautiously, knowing very well that she probably would have run to him when she had returned from Hong Kong. "But then there would have been the problem of getting you to believe me, wouldn't there?" she tacked on too sweetly.

That brought his midnight eyes to her profile in a quick, scorching glance. "If I'd been your friend I would have known Garrison and Prager weren't related to you," he said simply.

"Ah. The logic of the situation would have been clear right from the start, is that it? I understand. How much do you charge your friends for your assistance in situations like that? Is there a different rate from the one you charge Maddock, for example? Or strangers like Garrison and Prager? How do you work it, Judd? Do you have a sliding scale based on ability to pay?"

"Honor, shut up," he bit out savagely. "Just shut up or I'll lose my temper with you."

"I'm a little upset with you myself at the moment.

I've already lost my temper, in case you hadn't noticed!"

His hands tightened on the wheel but his driving remained smooth and controlled. "Was Melbourne trying to turn your 'friendship' back into something else? Does he want to sleep with you?"

"No!"

"Do you want to sleep with him?"

"Judd, I've told you, he's just a friend," she shot back in growing exasperation. "He was engaged to another friend of mine named Evie Newcomb. Before I left for Hong Kong they were having some problems. Today Steve called me up and said he and Evie were through and could he cry on my shoulder. I said yes. That's what friends are for, you see, Judd."

"Why did he break off his engagement? Does he want you back?"

"This is getting ridiculous! No, he did not end the engagement because of me! Evie got a job in Denver and left town."

"So?"

"So Steve has a job here in Phoenix. They've decided they can't stay engaged very easily when they're going to be living so far apart. There. That's the end of the story. Satisfied?"

"He should go to Denver and bring her home if he wants her."

"That sounds like a solid male viewpoint on the problem."

"What did you advise him to do?" he asked, sounding curious now.

"I advised him to go to Denver and get a job there so he could be with Evie."

To her great astonishment Judd seemed to consider that. "That's another possibility, I guess. In any event he shouldn't have been out crying on your shoulder tonight."

"Why not?" she demanded furiously.

"Because you belong to me," he retorted simply. "And I don't want other men crying on your shoulder."

"Damn it, Judd, how many times do I have to tell you that you don't own me just because you brought me out of Mexico!"

But he was concentrating on the airport turnoff and didn't bother to answer. Honor sat stiffly in her seat, her mind churning with possible ways of escape. When he parked the car she would be able to leap clear and make a dash toward the main terminal, perhaps. Or she could scream blue murder as he carried her through the general aviation flight lounge. Maybe a policeman would come along.

In the end none of those alternatives presented itself. Judd simply parked the car at the curb, scooped her up and carried her out onto the tarmac where rows of small private planes were sitting. He didn't even carry her through a waiting area. There was no one else around on the darkened tarmac.

Before Honor fully realized she wasn't going to have a chance to even attract attention with a good scream because of the noise of the jets taking off from the nearby commercial runway she found herself strapped into the passenger seat of the Cessna. In only a matter of moments Judd was receiving permission from the control tower to taxi out onto the runway. Honor sat raging helplessly in her seat, her bound hands useless in her lap. She found herself looking down at the receding lights of Phoenix as the Cessna leaped obediently into the air a few seconds later.

"What in hell do you think you're going to do with me in New Mexico?" she demanded above the roar of the engine.

"We're going to become friends," he told her and through her shock she was dimly aware that he meant every word.

"Judd, I hate to disillusion you, but good friendships don't start out like this!" She held up her bound wrists accusingly.

"Why don't you try to get some rest, Honor? It's a long trip."

Surprisingly enough she did manage to doze a little. The glow of the cabin lights and the steady throb of the engine were strangely lulling even though Honor had never been overly fond of flying. Perhaps she was just tired, or perhaps it was because, deep down, she trusted Judd's flying skills. Whatever the reason, when she awoke sometime later the Cessna was beginning to descend.

"Where are we?" she asked sleepily, lifting her hands to rub her eyes and discovering she was still bound. She lowered them again in disgust.

"Just outside of Albuquerque. A small airfield on the edge of the city."

"Are we landing for fuel?" she asked hopefully, plotting means of escape.

"No. We're home, Honor."

Home. "You live here in Albuquerque?"

"Yes."

The airstrip was deserted as the Cessna rolled to a stop at the far end. There was no chance of yelling for help, Honor acknowledged as Judd lifted her out of the cabin and set her on her feet. And she was too stiff from the long flight to make an attempt at running, she decided wretchedly. Honor watched as the plane was carefully put to bed for the night; this time she managed to resist any cracks about Judd's close association with his Cessna. Instinct told her he might not be in the best frame of mind for that kind of comment.

"Here, let me see your hands," he murmured gruffly as he finished chocking the wheels and came forward to take hold of her wrists. When she held them out stiffly he deftly untied the strip of fabric. "There's no place to run out here, honey," he advised, surveying her face in the glow of an overhead light. "The city is several miles away and there's nothing but desert in any other direction you care to look."

"You can't keep me here indefinitely, Judd, and you know it." She absently chafed her wrists, although they had not been bound very tightly.

"I know," was all he said and led her toward an open jeep that was parked beside one of the nearby buildings.

He drove only a short distance from the airport, pulling into the curving drive of what appeared to be a house done in the southwestern adobe style. There were no other houses close by, Honor observed uneasily as she climbed obediently out of the jeep and was led toward the front door. In the moonlight the adobe structure stood alone and aloof, rather like its owner.

"I haven't been here in a couple of weeks so there's probably not much to eat except whatever I left in the freezer. I can get you a drink, though," Judd began as he opened the door and urged Honor into the tiled hall.

She ignored the offer of a drink, glancing around quizzically. The house was a cool blend of colonial Mexican and local Indian colors and textures. The woven wall hangings were genuine, she saw at a glance, and Honor rather suspected that much of the heavy, carved furniture was, too. Large windows in the living room looked out into a private courtyard. A very self-contained sort of house, she thought. More refined and graceful than she would have expected, knowing what she did about the owner. Perhaps Judd had put into his house some of the things he couldn't put into his emotional life.

"Do you like it?" he asked from behind her and she spun around to find him watching intently as she surveyed his home.

"As prisons go, I suppose it's not bad. Did you bring me all this way to rape me in the comfort and convenience of your own home?" she mocked deliberately. Honor didn't like the way she had reacted to the question in his eyes. Damn it, she was not going to let herself be misled again by this man. He'd fooled her once by making her think he could be reached on a human level. He wouldn't fool her twice.

"Your room is down that hall," he told her, dark eyes hardening at the sharpness of her tongue.

"Fine. Then if you'll just hand me my suitcase I'll go to bed. It's been a very trying evening." Perhaps she could bluff her way through this, Honor decided on a small note of optimism.

He looked a little confused, as if things weren't

going quite according to plan. "A drink, first," he stated, heading toward the kitchen. "I'll fix us both a drink. We could use it."

As soon as he stepped around the corner and flipped on the kitchen light switch, Honor grabbed her suitcase and dashed down the hall to the room he had indicated would be hers. Once inside she whirled and slammed the door, locking it firmly behind her. Then, leaning back against it, she surveyed her quarters.

Not bad, actually, she decided wryly. Mexico had been a lot worse in terms of creature comforts. The windows looked out into the courtyard. There was a wide double bed with heavily carved posts at the far end of the room, and the rugs on the floor were beautiful examples of Indian weaving. Best of all there was a private bath, which she could see through a door that stood ajar. Straightening, she stalked across the room and checked to be sure the sliding glass doors were also locked.

It was a very masculine sort of room, she decided, experimentally opening a closet door. But that stood to reason. It was obvious Judd Raven didn't have much in the way of feminine influence in his life. She was just taking in the meaning of the shirts hanging in the closet when Judd's voice sounded grimly from the other side of the door.

"Honor! Stop acting like a child. Open the door. I've got a brandy for you."

"No, thanks." She peered more closely at the boots on the floor. Damn!

"Honor," he said again, sounding as if he were striving for patience, "you're in my room. Yours is the one across the hall."

Honor, having reached the same conclusion, swore softly again and shut the closet door. "I'm not coming out, Judd. I'm sure you can understand why. Sorry about the mixup in the rooms but I imagine you can make do. Good night!"

"Honor, I want to talk to you!"

"I'm not feeling chatty. Go hold one of your delightful single-word conversations with yourself!" She opened her suitcase and began fishing around for her nightgown and toothbrush. She was exhausted.

There was a long silence from the other side of the door and for an instant Honor almost felt guilty at having spoken so harshly. Immediately she scolded herself for the stupid reaction. What was the matter with her? The man had just kidnapped her, for God's sake!

She didn't actually hear him walk back down the hall. He moved too silently for that, but Honor's instincts told her when he was no longer standing on the other side of the door. Heaving a shaky sigh of relief, she made her way into the bathroom and began getting ready for bed. In the morning she would find a way of dealing with Judd Raven. Tonight she had been through too much. She needed her rest. With all the doors locked she felt safe enough to go to bed.

It must have been nearly two in the morning when Honor awoke in the middle of the wide bed to the realization that she was not alone in the room. For a disoriented moment she lay blinking in the darkness, trying to remember exactly where she was and why things weren't right.

Then she saw the dark, dangerous figure standing at

the foot of the bed and her sleep-bemused brain finally began to clear. She struggled up on the pillows with a gasp, her eyes wide and startled in the moonlight.

Judd watched her as she took in the sight of him standing so menacingly at the end of the bed. One hand rested on a high, carved bedpost and in the other he held a snifter of brandy. His eyes were gleaming jewels reflecting the silvery light of the moon as he stared down at her.

"You're sleeping in my bed," he drawled softly.

Honor stared at him, unable to move. In that moment she couldn't have fled, not even to save her own life. She could feel the waves of his desire fanning her like dark wings. The knowledge that he hovered so close sent a tremor through her but it was a tremor compounded as much of remembered passion as it was of fear. She had lain in Judd Raven's arms once before and it had been ecstasy. For some reason that seemed to be all her mind wanted to recall.

Still, a part of her refused to succumb so easily to the illusory love he offered. She would not be a victim again of her own romantic imagination. "No, Judd." The whispered denial came from between dry lips. Her whole mouth was suddenly dry. Awkwardly she touched the tip of her tongue to the corner of her lips. "No."

"But you are," he insisted far too gently. "You're sleeping in my bed. I've been sitting out in the front room thinking about it for an hour." He dropped his hand from the bedpost and paced a step closer, gazing down at her hungrily. "Why shouldn't I pick up where things went wrong? With you in my arms? You were happy that night, Honor. You couldn't have faked your response. I would have known. You wanted me that night as much as I wanted you."

"Judd," she said, careful to keep her voice very even. Was he drunk? "In the morning we can talk."

"It was in the morning that everything went wrong last time," he mused and came a pace closer. "It will be different this time. I want you to understand how it is for a man. . . ."

Her innate caution gave way to her remembered hurt and anger. "I've already learned how it is for a man," she bit out scathingly. "You made it very clear the last time. I don't want another lesson, Judd!"

"We're going to start over, Honor."

"No, not a chance." But of course that was why she was there, wasn't it? He was going to try to re-establish the physical relationship they had shared so briefly in Mexico. But why? Surely this man didn't lack for women when he wanted them. Hadn't he once told her he'd had a few interesting affairs?

"Yes," he countered, "we're going to start over and we're going to start at the point where everything went wrong last time. I want you to understand, this time. I want you to realize how I felt." He set down the brandy glass on the bedstand.

Honor drew in her breath, knowing her time had run out. Judd was intent on his purpose tonight. If she didn't make a move to run now it would be too late.

But even as she shoved back the bedclothes and scrambled for the far side, Honor knew deep inside that it was already too late. She didn't stand a chance.

He caught her before she had taken more than three running steps toward the sliding glass door, scooping her up in his arms and carrying her back to the bed. He dumped her into the middle of the rumpled bedclothes and before she could twist free he came down on top of her, anchoring her beneath him.

For a few moments she fought in blind panic, knowing it was hopeless and yet unable to think logically and conserve her energy. It was the same way it had been that first night in Mexico when she'd hurled herself at him in useless attack.

And just as he had that night, Judd restrained her without hurting her, using his crushing weight and superior strength to hold her flailing arms and pin her writhing legs until her energy waned.

"Let me go, Judd! *Let me go!*"

"Honor, stop fighting me. Please, stop fighting me," he muttered hoarsely and then with a low groan he bent his head and stilled her abruptly by taking her mouth with his own.

The shock of his warm, hungry mouth on hers washed through Honor like a tidal wave. Once again she felt the depths of his desire and her resistance faded in the face of it. He wanted her in a way no man had ever wanted her and there was no way she could ignore what that primitive passion did to her senses. No wonder she had longed for the physical relationship to mean something far more important to him. It had meant so much to her that her heart had refused at first to believe the feeling wasn't mutual.

"Let me have you, sweetheart," he growled against her lips. "Give yourself to me. I want you the way you were in Mexico, all soft and warm and clinging." He filled her mouth with his searching, exploring tongue, urging a response from the dark, warm depths of her. His legs stretched out alongside hers, the denim fabric of his jeans rough against her bare skin.

Honor felt her senses begin to spin and her emotions vacillated wildly from passion to anger and back again. "What do you want from me, damn you?" she cried, her head moving restlessly on the sheet.

"What does it look like?" he rasped. Then he buried his lips against her throat.

"You can get your sex from someone else. Leave me alone!"

"You don't understand! You didn't understand the morning we left Mexico and you don't understand now! But I'm going to show you what I mean this time."

She heard the resolute determination in his voice and knew, as she had known from the moment she saw him at the foot of her bed, that she was lost. He wasn't fighting her for the embrace, nor was he hurting her. Judd was simply intent on arousing her and she knew him well enough by now to know that there was little one could do to stop this man once he had set himself a course of action.

She was aware the instant he freed her hands to stroke the line of her thigh. She tried to push at him but already her body was succumbing to the demands of his. How could she resist the man she had thought herself falling in love with such a short time ago? How could she resist the desire in him? It reached out to envelop her, making her senses sing. She didn't hate Judd Raven. She could never hate him. He aroused her passion and her anger and even, at times, her compassion, but she would never be able to hate him. Especially not when he held her like this and made slow, intense love to her.

Slowly, slowly she stopped struggling, giving herself up to sweeping desire. He wanted her and she wanted him. Why did she have to look beyond that point? For now she would ignore the future and the past. Only the present counted.

She knew her implicit surrender must have been signaled immediately to Judd. Honor sensed the sigh of longing and satisfaction that seemed to emanate from deep in his chest as he gathered her closer.

"You won't regret it this time, sweetheart. This time you'll *understand!*" His hand slid along the naked length of her thigh, pushing up the hem of her cotton nightgown. "So soft, so sweet . . ."

Honor shuddered and her fingers lifted to twine themselves in the depths of his black-and-silver hair. The feel of it was excruciatingly exciting and she moaned softly. Everything about him excited her. The musky, warm scent of his body was intoxicating and the roughness of his unshaven cheek made her twist with a new kind of restlessness.

"Judd, I shouldn't let you do this to me. Not again."

"This time it will be different," he vowed thickly. "God, I've been wanting you so, Honor. Did you really think I could let you go? When I saw you with that other man tonight I wanted to break his neck!"

"And me?" she dared, driven by her own rising passion to taunt him as she had done so often down in Mexico. "What were you going to do to me?"

"Exactly what I did do. Kidnap you and bring you home with me. Hell, lady, you have the power to drive me out of my mind!" He shifted abruptly, tearing impatiently at the buttons of his dark shirt. His eyes burned into her face as he stripped the garment from his body and then reached down to unfasten his jeans.

A moment later he lay naked beside her, his hand playing with the skirt of the nightgown while his lips explored the curve of her shoulder. Honor shut her eyes, letting herself thrill to the power he had over her body. She clutched at the thrusting line of his back as he slowly worked the nightgown up over her hips.

"Oh, Judd!"

He flattened his palm on her thigh, smoothing her skin as if it were priceless silk. Then he lifted her slightly and pulled the nightgown off completely. "Sweetheart . . . !" he breathed as he tossed the light cotton garment heedlessly down onto the floor. He lowered his head to taste the budding nipple of her breast and she trembled with pleasure as he made her softness swell.

When her legs moved, seeking his, Judd trailed his palm down the curve of her stomach and boldly found the soft mound below. Honor moaned his name aloud and clung more tightly than ever, arching her lower body into the warmth of his hand.

Slowly, with infinite sensitivity, Judd traced an erotic path to the hot, damp warmth between her legs. With his knee he opened her thighs to his touch and when she shivered he soothed her with dark, persuasive words that urged her to relax and let him fly away with her. Or at least that was how her enthralled mind interpreted the words.

Her nails began to sink tantalizingly into his shoulders and Judd's response was a low, aching groan that spoke clearly of his barely restrained need. The part of her that always seemed inclined to tease and taunt him drove her to seek a further reaction. She loved getting a reaction, any kind of reaction, from him, Honor realized vaguely. Something in her seized on such slim evidence and pretended it was meaningful communication.

"Love me, Judd," she whispered, making no attempt to hide the arousal in her voice. It would have been pointless. He must know the effect he was having on her body. "Make love to me, darling."

She knew even as she spoke that love was not a word in his vocabulary but she used it anyway, as if daring him to deny that he wasn't making love to her. He wouldn't, she told herself. He wanted her too badly now to jeopardize her willing surrender with an argument over the word she was using to describe it.

And she was right. He didn't correct her, he simply ignored the word "love" altogether. Instead he asked her for the words he wanted. "Tell me you need me, sweetheart," he coaxed roughly as he dropped tiny, stinging kisses into the pit of her stomach. "Tell me how much you want me."

"I want you, Judd. Oh, God, how I want you." She slipped her hands along his back down to the hard, muscular male buttocks. His savagely indrawn breath was music to her.

"Yes," he muttered huskily. "Oh, yes, sweetheart. Touch me. Pull me into you. Show me you want me."

Sensuously he stroked the inside of her leg down to her knee and back until she flexed it in an agony of desire. "Now, Judd. Please, *now!*"

He didn't answer, moving aggressively over her instead until he lay along the length of her slender body. Honor felt gloriously crushed and reveled in the sensual weight of him. When he inserted his legs between hers she obeyed the silent command and opened herself to him.

It was as he hesitated a moment longer, seeking to

arouse her to a fever pitch of wanting, that she was assailed by a lingering sense of vulnerability. She could feel the waiting heat of his manhood pressing close and all at once a vision of the future infiltrated her mind. For just an instant she saw herself as she had been that last morning in Mexico, hurt, angry and weak.

As if he could read her mind, Judd was suddenly grating harsh words against her lips. "No," he ordered fiercely. "No, don't go cold on me now. It's too late. You've already given yourself tonight!" Then he moved against her softness, filling her completely in a hard, incredibly exciting way that literally deprived her of breath.

By the time she regained the air in her lungs Honor was already caught up in the dizzying spiral of Judd's passion. He reached down to hold her hips more firmly to him, forcing her into the thrilling pattern of the rhythm he was creating. Helplessly, heedlessly, she clung to him as if to a huge, soaring bird. There amid the dangerous peaks at the top of the world he was her only source of safety.

Relentlessly he carried them higher until at last Honor could go no further. She felt the sweeping tremors pour through her body and knew that Judd was as violently aware of her response as she herself was. She heard him say her name over and over again as she collapsed mindlessly in his arms and then he was following her over the edge and she held him tightly as he shuddered heavily and then lay still.

It was a long time before Honor emerged from the mists to become faintly aware of a gentle movement against the inside of her wrist. Opening her eyes she turned her head on the pillow and found Judd lying beside her, his fingers gliding back and forth across the scar that looked so much like a botched attempt at suicide. He stared at her as she regarded him from beneath half-closed lashes.

"Tell me about this," he demanded softly.

She hesitated, aware of the drying perspiration on his sleek, lean body and of how uncompromisingly male he was in his nakedness. Hard and tough and aggressive. Not at all the sort of gentle, sensitive man she had once dreamed of falling in love with. What had she done?

"Honor, tell me about the scar."

She blinked. "That night in Hong Kong—the night I found out what Garrison and Prager were really up to—it happened then," she said softly, the memory still unnerving her. "When I realized that Nick had seen me, I knew I had to run. I found a cab which took me to the hotel. I had it wait while I collected my passport and the tickets. I had all of the tickets, Leo's and Nick's as well as my own. I took them, hoping it would slow them down. Even with connections it takes a while to buy international air tickets. Luckily there was a flight out that night that I could get on. They had second-guessed me, though. They arrived at the airport a few minutes behind me. I just kept myself hidden in the crowd. There wasn't much they could do. But Nick spotted me when I ran to catch my plane. I'd deliberately waited until the last second, so I could stay hidden as long as possible."

"Keep going."

Honor shook her head helplessly. "He swung his arm as I raced past him. I thought he was trying to grab me and I dodged. I didn't realize until the last instant that he had a small knife in his hand. I guess he thought if he could stab me quickly he could just pretend I'd fainted in his arms. But when I dodged aside, the knife tip caught on my bracelet. It was a chain-link thing and it snagged the blade for a few seconds. The bracelet came off and I kept going until I was safe behind the 'passengers only' sign. A few minutes later I was on the plane and they were helpless to stop me."

She shuddered. "I only realized I was bleeding when I got on the plane."

"I knew there had to be a good explanation." He sighed and leaned back against the pillows.

"Did you?" she challenged huskily.

"You may be a romantic but you're too gutsy to resort to something like a suicide attempt!" Judd closed his eyes, continuing to hold her wrist loosely in his palm. "Prager was sure there would be some mark on your wrist, so I guess he knew he'd cut you. The bastard. He and Garrison sure knew how to dovetail that little snippet of information into the total story they gave me."

"Yes." She lay watching him, wishing she had ESP. What in the world was he thinking?

"I shouldn't have come in here tonight," he said as if answering her silent question. He put his arm across his eyes. "I didn't plan to, you know."

Honor went very still. "Didn't you?" She could hardly breathe.

He shook his head and lowered his arm to stare at her still, tense face. "No. It was the thought of the way you had run in here, locking the door on me. My own door! And I'd found you with that other man tonight after looking for you all day in Phoenix. Then there was that long, tiring flight. And a couple of brandies. What with one thing and another, I guess I lost control. But you don't have to worry. It won't happen again. This isn't the way to go about putting things right and I know it."

Honor swallowed. "What exactly do you want to put right, Judd?"

"Honor, you misunderstood everything that morning we left Mexico. I know I didn't come through as your ideal of a romantic hero. I realize you woke up with some rosy image of me that I promptly failed to live up to. I handled everything badly, but I could only think of one thing and that was to get the whole damn mess straightened out. I wasn't thinking in terms of wine and roses and undying love. I just wanted to get you out of Mexico and out of the mess in which you'd found yourself. I'm sorry, honey, but one night in bed with you wasn't enough to answer all the questions that had been raised. Maybe I should have instantly believed your tale. Maybe one of your 'friends' would have believed it without question. But I've been living by myself for a long time. I'm not used to placing unquestioning trust in another human being. I had to find out for myself what was going on."

"So I gathered," she managed faintly. And he wasn't accustomed to falling in love, either, she decided silently. He probably didn't even have the vaguest idea of how to go about doing that. "What happens now, Judd?" she asked starkly.

"Now we start over. You belong to me, Honor. I realize I'm not what you've been looking for in a man. You've made it damn clear you think I'm a mercenary bastard who knows nothing about the sensitive side of life. And you're probably right. But I'm not going to let you walk out on me again. Do you understand?"

"You can't keep me here indefinitely against my will, Judd," she pointed out carefully, at a loss to comprehend her own feelings in that moment.

He touched the side of her face with rough fingers. "I only have to keep you here long enough to convince you that you have to stay," he said simply.

"I'm not staying with you, Judd. I won't live with a man who doesn't know the meaning of love." She met his eyes unflinchingly, refusing to give way beneath the grim determination she read in his gaze.

"You have to give me a chance, Honor," he said softly.

"Why?"

"Because you're too soft, too gentle, not to give me a chance now that you're no longer blazingly angry with me." He rolled off the edge of the bed and got to his feet. "Good night, sweetheart. I'll see you in the morning."

Honor stared after him in confusion as Judd quietly let himself out of the room.

Chapter 9

THE NEXT MORNING WARINESS REPLACED THE CONFUSION Honor had been feeling during the night. It was an innate, feminine caution and it was again tinged with resentment. But as she climbed out of bed and padded over to the window a lot of the feelings of anger were directed at herself.

How could she have been so weak as to let herself be seduced by Judd Raven a second time? There wasn't another man on the face of the earth who could have managed to do that to her! What was it about this one?

Several birds had landed in the courtyard garden and in the bright, early-morning light they hopped cheerfully about having breakfast. These were cute little creatures, though, not menacing birds of prey. They feasted on berries and seeds and warbled sweetly. If a raven had appeared in their midst they would have scattered in a flash.

Her mouth curving wryly, Honor turned away from the window and started toward the bath. She could feel the memory of the night imprinted on her body. There was a lingering, tantalizing ache in the muscles of her thighs and it seemed to Honor she could vividly remember the sheer weight of the man who had swept her away in the darkness.

What was she going to do?

A shower made her feel somewhat revitalized and by the time she emerged from it the aroma of sizzling bacon did its share to lift her spirits. Judd was cooking breakfast.

But by the time she had dressed in a pair of jeans and a long-sleeved checked shirt with a mandarin collar, Honor was no nearer a solution about how she should handle the situation. Clipping her amber hair at the nape of her neck, she slipped into a pair of sandals and let herself out of the room.

She could, in the light of day, simply demand to be released or threaten to call the police. Would that faze Judd? She remembered that he had seemed unintimidated by Craig Maddock and decided that calling the cops might not make much of an impression on her captor.

She could try running again. Her mouth twisted in disgust. Fat lot of good that would do if Judd decided to come after her, which he undoubtedly would.

She could try screaming for help every time they came within earshot of a stranger. *If* they came within earshot of any passing strangers.

Or she could give Judd his chance. What Honor

didn't quite understand was what he intended to prove. She wasn't sure he did, either.

But he had given her a chance in Mexico. He had allowed her four extra days and during that time she had managed to at least put a few doubts in his head about Garrison and Prager. If she hadn't been given that chance, she might very well be dead by now. Judd hadn't trusted her completely or lost his heart to her or anything else so dramatic, but he had at least checked out a portion of her story and his willingness to do that had saved her life.

How much did she really owe him?

Honor had the uncomfortable realization that she owed Judd Raven her life.

It was on that thought that she entered the kitchen and discovered she was hungry. Judd was in the act of stacking bacon on a hot platter as she walked cautiously through the door. He glanced up quickly, the expression in his dark eyes almost as wary as her own.

"Breakfast." He nodded toward the bacon and a large stack of toast.

"Yes." Honor surveyed the huge pile of bacon. "Who else is invited? There's enough there to feed a platoon."

"I'm not used to cooking for two," he muttered. "Besides, I seem to remember you had a pretty healthy appetite down in Mexico." He looked down at the bacon and toast. "This was about all there was in the freezer."

Why was she feeling an insane urge to show some appreciation of his efforts? "It looks delicious. I'm starving." Going forward she reached out and helped herself to a strip of bacon. Judd looked visibly re-

lieved and Honor didn't know whether to be furious
with herself for softening or to give in to the small
feeling of pleasure she got out of making him happy.

Wordlessly they sat down at the small kitchen table
and began eating. Honor refused to meet Judd's eyes
for several moments, her own uncertainty and caution
making her uncomfortable. It was he who finally
broke the silence between them, extending a hand to
touch her scarred wrist.

"Honor." He waited until she finally looked up and
then he went on very intently. "I know I handled
things badly last night."

"That's putting it mildly," she managed with a
flippancy she was far from feeling. "Kidnapping is a
Federal crime, you know."

He shook his head impatiently. "I don't mean in
bringing you here. I mean in coming to your bed last
night. I honestly hadn't intended to do that. But
sometimes you have a way of making me do things I
don't intend to do," he concluded bluntly.

"So it's all my fault?"

Judd stared at her. "Maybe it would be better if we
talked about something else," he finally decided. It
was abruptly obvious that he was backing away from
the issue.

"Such as?" she challenged bravely. Judd backing
down? Amazing!

"Such as what we're going to do today," he announced, removing his hand from her wrist and
picking up another slice of bacon. He seemed bound
and determined to lighten his tone and the mood in
the kitchen. "I thought we could have some fun
together."

It was Honor's turn to stare, this time suspiciously.

"Fun?" She wasn't at all convinced Judd Raven knew the meaning of the word. She had a clear memory of trying to teach him to play down in Mexico. The effort had wound up with her getting dunked in the stream.

"I," he told her rather grandly, "am going to give you your first flying lesson." He waited for her to show her unabashed delight.

Honor blinked at him. "A flying lesson?" she finally repeated weakly.

"You're going to love it," he assured her, gaining enthusiasm rapidly as he talked. "It's a whole different world when you're at the controls of an airplane. And flying is something we can do together."

Together. Honor rolled the word around in her head. What was Judd trying to do? Was flying his idea of fun? Was he trying to extend to her the bridge of mutual play that she had once extended to him? If that was the case, Honor realized, she didn't have the heart to turn him down. It was very clear to her that this man had almost no experience at playing with another human being. But she also wasn't at all sure a flying lesson was the proper way for him to begin. She remembered her first driving lesson. It had not been fun.

Having made up his mind, however, Judd was not about to be dissuaded. Immediately after breakfast Honor found herself being driven back out to the small airport where they had landed the previous evening. This morning she noticed a few other small planes tied down near the old hangar and there were half a dozen men hanging around.

They greeted Judd as he arrived with Honor in tow. He nodded familiarly but made no effort to pause long enough to introduce Honor. Instead he got right to the business of refueling the Cessna and Honor found herself obliged to follow every step he made. Her lesson, it seemed, was going to begin on the ground.

By the time she had been walked through the preflight check of the aircraft and found herself strapped into the pilot's seat, her head was already spinning with the number of complex instruments, facts and details Judd was blithely explaining.

"Are you sure I should start off in the pilot's seat?" she asked as he got in on the passenger side.

"Sure. I've got a duplicate set of controls over here. Don't worry. Now at a small airport like this where there is no control tower we all use one frequency on the radio. Every pilot approaching or leaving the airport announces his location so others will know where to look for him in the sky. Okay, here you go. Here's the key."

He handed it to her as if handing her the keys to a treasure chest. Honor took it gingerly, feeling more apprehensive by the minute. "Aren't I going to just sort of sit here and watch?"

"Nope. You're going to fly us right off the runway. Don't worry, it's a cinch. This baby practically takes off by itself."

"Uh-huh. Look, Judd—"

"Over there is the master switch," he interrupted, and went on from there to give her a brief resume of the takeoff procedure. As he lectured, Honor's palms began to grow damp; the checked shirt was already beginning to cling to her skin.

The next thing she knew she was actually guiding the Cessna out onto the taxiway. The plane didn't seem to want to go in a straight line.

"A tailwheel plane is a little hard to steer on the ground," Judd said firmly. "You have to correct for the torque of the engine. *You do it with the rudder pedals,*" he added quickly, his voice hardening. An instant later he, himself, hit the rudder pedals on his side of the aircraft to straighten out the weaving Cessna. Honor wasn't certain but she thought the action was accompanied by a muffled oath. Her palms grew damper as she gripped the steering yoke.

Then she was at the end of the runway, pointing into the wind. Nervously she followed Judd's crisp directions, opening the throttle until the little craft was racing down the pavement. She was dimly aware of the fact that Judd was having to continue using the rudder to keep the Cessna in a straight line and then, before she quite realized it, the plane was off the ground.

The ease with which it all happened took her by surprise. Before she could adjust to being in flight Judd was calling out directions. His voice became harder and grimmer as the seconds ticked past.

"Get the nose down! We're not doing aerobatics out here! Watch the rate-of-climb indicator. We only want to go up at about eight hundred feet per minute. You'll stall out if you go up too fast."

Which one of the many instruments was the rate-of-climb indicator? She'd forgotten already. Honor was searching frantically for it when Judd interrupted roughly. "Okay, now start your turn. *Like this.*" He grabbed the controls and corrected for her too-rapid maneuver. Again she thought she heard another stifled swear word. When the turn was completed and they were flying toward the distant mountains, he released the controls again.

Just as Honor nervously took them over the radio
chattered. "What's that?" she demanded.

"Another pilot telling us he's a couple of miles from
the field. A Piper Cherokee. See? He's at three
o'clock."

Honor stared blankly around, wondering which
direction was three o'clock. "No, I don't see him.
Judd, is he close to us?" Vivid images of midair
collisions assailed her. *Where is he?*

"At three o'clock," Judd repeated impatiently.
"Over there. For crying out loud, Honor, can't you
see him?"

"That little white speck?"

"Yes, damn it. Hey, keep the wings level!"

"It's hard to tell what's level up here in the air," she
protested.

"Then take a look at the artificial horizon," he
ordered, tapping the glass face of another instrument.
"What in hell do you think it's for?"

"How should I know? Judd, maybe you'd better
take over. . . ."

"No, by God. You're going to learn to fly this thing
if it kills me. Okay, level off, we're high enough. Not
so fast! Ease off on the throttle. We don't need all that
power to fly straight and level. Slowly, Honor, *slowly*.
Don't yank the throttle out like that."

The plane suddenly seemed to sink several feet in
the sky. Honor panicked. "What was that? What
happened?"

"Just a little turbulence. Nothing to worry about.
Now, see that peak over there? Try flying toward it.
Remember, keep the wings level. What the devil?
Honor, the airspeed's disintegrating. It's going to hell!
Get the nose down, you idiot, or we'll stall. For God's

sake, can't you feel that shudder? That's the first warning of a stall. *Get the damned nose down!*" He grabbed the controls again and eased the plane back into a level altitude.

"I don't know about this, Judd. . . ."

"Don't steer with the rudder pedals," he growled.

"You did on the ground!"

"That's different. Okay, let's try another turn. Easy, Honor, take it *easy!* You want to get us into a spin? Watch the turn-and-bank indicator."

"Oh, boy, am I having fun," Honor muttered savagely just under her breath.

"What?" He glared at her suspiciously.

"Nothing. Forget it."

"All right, now let's try to keep to one altitude, shall we?" Judd asked with exaggerated patience. "We're all over the sky. Watch the altimeter for a minute, will you?"

"Which one's the altimeter?"

"This one!"

"There certainly are a lot of instruments, aren't there?" Honor gritted tightly, staring at the numbers behind the glass in front of her. "This isn't exactly like driving a car."

"Of course it isn't. Keep the wings level, Honor."

The next half hour comprised the worst thirty minutes Honor had ever spent in her life. She was soaking wet by the time Judd instructed her to turn the plane back toward the airport. Her instructor sat grim and implacable beside her, his vocabulary now consisting of a heartfelt oath every three words or so.

Honor felt like doing more than a little swearing herself. She didn't care if she never rode in a plane again in her life. Some fun.

"Okay, we're nearing the airport. I'll take over," Judd announced, sounding as relieved as Honor felt when he took the controls. "You can handle the radio."

"I don't know what to say!"

"I'll tell you what to say and when to say it," he informed her evenly. "Start by saying, 'This is Cessna nine-nine Lima five miles out. . . .' "

Honor seized the microphone and dutifully repeated the landing information in a laconic, laid-back, southwestern twang that brought Judd's head around in astonishment.

"Where the hell did you get the accent?" he demanded.

"All pilots talk like that on the radio," she informed him sweetly. "Everyone knows that. Commercial pilots, airline pilots, private pilots, astronauts, military pilots. They all develop this lovely southwestern drawl when they get on the radio. Haven't you ever seen the movies? Or heard astronauts landing? It's part of having the *right stuff,* you know. Even you talk like that on the microphone, Judd."

"I talk like that because I was born and raised in the Southwest! It's my natural accent!"

"Nope. You talk like that on the radio because that's the way pilots are supposed to talk. What do I say next?" she inquired, feeling more cheerful by the minute now that the controls had been taken out of her hands. "I like this part. Maybe I could just become a professional on the mike."

Judd cast pleading eyes toward heaven but he grimly gave her the rest of the directions, wincing visibly as she repeated them in her newfound accent.

"Cessna nine-nine Lima entering downwind for

runway one-eight," she drawled at the appropriate moment. "Turning final . . ."

Judd brought the Cessna down with his usual expertise, allowing the rollout to bring them even with one of the runway turnoffs. It had been a perfect flareout and landing, and Honor was disgusted by it. The least he could have done was to have bumped along the runway a bit. He was just trying to make her own performance in the air suffer by comparison. "Show off," she muttered.

"All right, now, Honor. Pay attention. There's a lot to be done at the end of the flight. You have to pull the mixture control, turn off the mag switches, lock the controls, shut off the radios and the master switch—"

"You should make a list!" she told him crisply.

"I've got a list," he countered. "Right here." He reached behind his seat and produced a plastic-encased list of procedures to be followed before takeoff and after landing.

"Well, why in hell didn't you give that to me earlier?" she blazed. "It would have made things much simpler."

"I thought it would just confuse you. I wanted your first time up in the air to be simple and fun."

"Let me tell you, Judd Raven, I haven't had this much fun since the night my car broke down on a deserted highway and I had to figure out how to work a jack for the first time in my life! On second thought, I had a lot *more* fun that night because at least no one was around to yell at me!"

"I didn't yell at you!" he shouted as he brought the Cessna to a smart stop beside the old hangar. "I was giving you directions."

Honor opened the door on her side of the cabin, unfastened her seat belt and jumped out onto the pavement. "You give directions with all the patience and finesse of a stampeding buffalo! I feel as if I got trampled up there in the air!" She plucked at her perspiration-dampened shirt. "Just look at me. I was a nervous wreck. You're supposed to go slowly when you teach someone something so complicated. Even my father had more patience when he taught me to drive a car and God knows he never had much patience with me!"

"I'm not your father, damn it!" Judd finished shutting down the Cessna and leaped out onto the pavement, striding around to confront her. "This is something we're going to do together. I want you to be good at it. After all, my life is going to be in your hands during the times you're at the controls! And what about your own neck? Don't you want to know what you're doing when you're up there?"

"And let's not forget the precious airplane, either," she came back roundly. "We both know how you feel about that Cessna. If I were to damage it—"

"I'd take a horsewhip to you if you ever damaged my airplane!" he vowed in a thundering voice that she had never before heard from him. Judd Raven was definitely not in full control of himself. He faced her with his hands clenched into fists on his hips, dark eyes glaring and hard mouth set in a taut line.

"See what I mean?" Honor nodded her head in defiant vindication. "That proves it. You care more about the damned airplane than you do anything else, including my feelings! You don't shout at that Cessna the way you're shouting at me!"

A few of the men who had been hanging around the

field when Judd and Honor had arrived began taking an interest in the brawl that seemed to be developing before their very eyes. Lounging against the old metal frame of the hangar building, they pulled their caps down low over their eyes and watched in growing amusement.

"If I hadn't shouted at you a couple of times up there you would have tried to kill us!" Judd rasped furiously.

"I respond much better to calm, polite instructions. But you never tried that technique, did you? From the moment we got in the plane you began hammering away at me, telling me what to do."

"Well someone had to tell you what to do! What did you think? That you were going to get into the plane and fly it all by yourself without any help?"

"I needed a little professional instruction. Not a lot of yelling and screaming! I knew this was a bad idea. I knew it this morning when you first suggested it, but I was willing to give it a try. Let me tell you something, Judd Raven. You may find all this a lot of fun but to me it was sheer torture! Furthermore, the way I feel right now I don't ever intend to get back into the cockpit of an airplane with you again. At least not until you learn a little self-control in the air!"

"Honor!" Judd abruptly slid a seething glance toward the small gaggle of men hovering just within earshot. "Come on, let's go home. We can discuss this some other time!" He reached out to grab her arm but Honor stepped back hurriedly.

"Oh, no, you don't! I'm not even sure I want to get into a car with you right away! Who knows? You may feel I need a little instruction in driving or something. I don't think my nerves could take much more today!"

"Honor, you're being ridiculous!" he grated and in the bright desert sunlight she could have sworn that the high bones of his cheeks were stained with red.

Was she embarrassing him in front of his fellow pilots? Honor wondered, relishing the prospect of a little revenge. After all, Judd deserved some recompense for what he had just put her through in the Cessna. "Tell me what else you do for fun around here," she invited scathingly, gesturing vaguely at the rest of the airfield. "Dogfights over Albuquerque? Near-misses with some of the commercial liners landing at the big airport in town? Do you give tourists hair-raising flights over the mountains? Boy, this world of flying sure is some fun! A laugh a minute!"

"Damn it, Honor!" Judd stepped toward her. The glitter in his eyes should have warned her, but Honor plunged on recklessly.

"You sure had a good idea when you decided to take me flying this morning, Judd. I want you to know that I shall never forget the experience. I can see right now what a real togetherness sort of sport this is. What I want to know is, at what point do I get to start yelling at you? Or is that always going to be a one-way street? Will I always be the one who gets yelled at because I'll always be the one with the least experience? I'm going to tell you right now, Judd, that doesn't sound like a whole lot of *fun* to me!"

At that moment she suddenly realized she'd pushed him too far. Judd moved, swooping down on her with the speed and coordination of his namesake.

"Judd! Stop it!"

In the next instant she was over his shoulder and being hauled unceremoniously toward the waiting jeep. After the initial shock, laughter began to well up inside her. Did he think she was defeated? She still had a couple of shots left and she meant to take them.

"Do you know what he's doing?" she asked, calling out to the grinning men by the hangar. "He's playing a game. It's the only game he knows. Judd has a very limited repertoire, you see. Actually he didn't know any games at all until I taught him this one. It's called Taming the Shrew. One of these days I'm going to teach him another sort of game. Maybe something to do with cards. Checkers, perhaps," she went on musingly as Judd reached the jeep and tossed her lightly down onto the seat. She subsided in a grinning heap of tousled femininity as he climbed into the seat beside her and swiveled to face her with an expression that threatened disaster.

"What the hell are you laughing at?" he gritted.

"You."

"You enjoyed that little scene back there in front of those men?"

"Well, it had its moments. And you have to admit I deserved something for the treatment I'd taken up there in the air," she told him complacently.

He glowered at her for a split second and then something unfamiliar appeared in the depths of his eyes, an expression Honor had only seen once before in Judd. The other time had been when he'd dunked her and his shirts into the stream. Judd's gaze was actually mirroring rueful laughter.

"You were madder than a wet hen by the time we landed, weren't you?" he finally asked slowly.

"Judd, you started yelling at me before we even got off the ground! Sitting with you through half an hour of your 'instruction' would be enough to put most people off flying for life!"

"Was it really that bad?" he asked wistfully.

"It was."

He shook his head wryly. "It worked both ways you know. I was a nervous wreck by the time we got back on the ground. I've never tried to teach someone to fly before. All of a sudden I have a lot more respect for professional instructors. But, Honor, I honestly didn't intend for things to wind up this way."

"I know. You wanted me to have fun."

"That's exactly what I wanted. I thought if you learned to love flying you'd want to spend more time with me. But the only part you enjoyed was yelling at me after we got back down, wasn't it?"

Suddenly Honor couldn't resist the overwhelming urge to offer some reassurance. "Judd," she murmured, impulsively putting her hand on his arm, "teaching someone to fly is like teaching someone to drive. You shouldn't even attempt it if you're too close to the other person. It takes a certain professional distance. That much is obvious. If you really want me to learn to fly you'd be better off lining up a certified flight instructor for me and turning me over to him for the basics."

He searched her face. "I got the feeling you weren't ever going to go up again. At least not willingly."

"People say a lot of things in the heat of battle," she said offhandedly. "Things they may not mean to be taken literally."

"You'd still be willing to try learning? If someone else were to do the teaching, that is?"

She shrugged. "I might be willing to give it a shot."

He hesitated, the fingers of one bronzed hand lightly tapping the wheel in an uncharacteristic movement. "There's just one thing, Honor."

"Ummm?"

"Even if you got your license and even if you got very good in the air, every time you went up with me I'd still be the pilot in command. I'm too used to being in charge of my own plane. I'd let you do some of the flying but I can't guarantee I wouldn't still yell at you from time to time."

"I'll just bet you can't guarantee it."

He frowned. "That doesn't bother you?"

"Not as long as I get a chance to yell back once we're on the ground," she said, grinning.

"Like you did a few minutes ago? Hell, I'm not sure I could take too much of that! Those guys are going to be laughing their fool heads off every time someone mentions this morning's little fiasco!"

"Keep it in mind when you're yelling at me in the air."

"That sounds suspiciously like blackmail to me."

"Yes, it does, doesn't it?"

He paused again and Honor knew he was trying to work something through in his head. "Do you really think the lesson didn't work out because I'm too close to you?" he finally asked quietly.

"I'm sure of it," she retorted dryly. And she knew it was the truth. Whatever the status of their relationship there was no way of denying that the relationship, itself, existed. They were not mere acquaintances. They were a man and a woman who had been through several dramatic, emotional days together.

Judd stared at her for a long moment and then drew a deep breath. "In that case, I guess I don't mind so much that everything went haywire this morning. If you're feeling that close to me already, maybe we're making some progress."

"Progress toward what, Judd?" she asked very soberly.

"Toward becoming friends."

"Is that really what you want from me? Friendship?"

"You know damn good and well it's not all I want, but it's part of it." He threw open the door of the jeep again and jumped out. "Come on, I'm going to have to face this sooner or later so I might as well get it over with as fast as possible." He took her arm and started resolutely back toward the hangar.

"Where are we going now?" she asked in confusion.

"I'm going to introduce you to a few of the guys who have planes here at the field. The audience in front of which you just performed so brilliantly," he added in a laconic drawl. "I know they'll be dying of curiosity."

Honor arched an eyebrow. "Curiosity about me? You don't often take women flying?"

"No," he said shortly, "I don't."

Honor took pleasure in that information. By the time Judd had drawn her near the hangar and had begun making introductions she was smiling quite brilliantly.

"Pleased to meetcha, ma'am."

"Take it you had an interesting flight, Miss Knight?"

"We don't often see Judd, here, so *excited*, so to speak. You must have given him a real nice tour of Albuquerque from the air."

Judd interrupted at this point to note blandly, "She scared the living daylights out of me. But she's got good instincts. With a little training she'll make a good pilot."

"Thought you looked a trifle green when you got out of the plane, Judd," one of the men noted commiseratingly. "And I know I ain't never heard you yell at anyone like that before. Especially a female!"

Judd took the ribbing with surprisingly good grace. Honor, who forgot she should have been asking for help in escaping from him instead of wasting time taunting her captor, found herself laughing out loud more than once. It was very obvious Judd wasn't accustomed to being the center of so much teasing attention. The fact that he was tolerating it now did not go unnoticed by the surrounding men.

"You thinking of giving the little lady any more lessons, Judd?" asked one wearing the overalls of a crop duster.

"I think any more lessons from me would have us at each other's throats before we could get the plane back on the ground," Judd admitted blandly, glancing at Honor. "I found out this morning that you can't give lessons to someone if you're too close to her, you see."

"Got a point there," another man observed. "Tried to teach my wife to fly. Nearly drove us to the divorce courts. Farm her out to a professional instructor. Much easier on your nerves, Judd."

"The funny thing is," the crop duster said with a glance at Judd, "I never even suspected that Raven *had* nerves. Not until I saw him leap out of that plane and start yelling at the little lady here a few minutes ago."

"He lost his temper," Honor explained far too kindly. Her eyes were brimming with laughter as she looked at Judd.

"Another first. Never saw Raven lose his temper before, either," the crop duster mused with a wide grin. "You must really have a powerful effect on him, ma'am."

Judd lifted one dark brow with an air of cool superiority. "Honor and I tend to rile each other on occasion. It's because we're so *close,* I suppose."

"Not quite as close as he and the Cessna are, naturally," Honor interposed dryly. "But, then, I realize that's a very special sort of relationship."

Judd's eyes narrowed as the others chuckled in appreciation, and for an instant Honor wished she'd kept her mouth shut. From the very beginning Judd hadn't liked her caustic remarks about his relationship with the plane.

Then quite suddenly he was laughing. Honor stood staring in absolute amazement, realizing it was the only time she had ever heard him laugh. It was a deep, warm, vibrant sound that seemed to come from far down in his chest and it did something strange and wonderful to her senses. A moment later, she was joining him, and for the first time since she had met him Honor knew the fundamental pleasure of laughing out loud with the man she loved.

Chapter 10

SHE LOVED HIM. HONOR CAUTIOUSLY ABSORBED THE information into her system as if it were a potentially dangerous narcotic. She loved Judd Raven. She'd probably been in love with him ever since that first time they had slept together in Mexico. Perhaps earlier. The knowledge explained so much: why she had been so angry the morning he had announced he was taking her back to the States, her strange sense of vulnerability around him, and the unbelievable gladness she had experienced when he did something as simple as sharing her laughter.

"Honor?" Judd's questioning voice interrupted her thoughts as they drove back down the road from the airfield.

"Hmmmm?" The warm wind whipped her hair as the jeep swept along the highway. She didn't look at him.

"What are you thinking? You've been awfully quiet for a while," he complained gruffly. "Are you still upset about the flying lesson?" he added uneasily.

"No. I was thinking of something else," she responded evenly. "I was thinking about how long I'll be staying here with you in Albuquerque."

There was silence from the driver's seat for a critical minute and then Judd asked with surprising calm, "And how long is that?"

"Four days." She turned her head to look at him. "That's how long you gave me down in Mexico, Judd. Four days. I owe you my life. If you hadn't gotten me out of Mexico, sooner or later Garrison and Prager would have sent someone who might have had fewer scruples than you did. I can't repay you for my life so I'll give you the four days you originally granted me. Fair enough?" It was an ultimatum of sorts and they both knew it. Honor waited uneasily for his reaction.

Judd slid her a cool, unreadable glance. "We'll talk about it at the end of the four days."

As a response it was a little unsatisfactory, but Honor told herself she was dealing with a complicated situation and a complex man. She mustn't expect Judd to react in predictable, conventional ways. He lived by his own rules. "Where are we going now?" she asked as coolly as possible.

"To the store. That bacon and toast was the last edible stuff I had in the house."

Four days, he thought, aware of a sudden sensation of being trapped; of time running out. Four days. She was right. It was what he had given her down in Mexico. There was a certain justice to the ultimatum but he refused to tell himself he would abide by it. Four days was so little time!

He had known from the beginning that he couldn't really keep her long against her will. They both knew it. But he needed time. Was this how she had felt down in Mexico when she had been frantically trying to convince him that she was in real danger? Judd realized abruptly that he was gritting his teeth and forced himself to relax. He'd take it one day at a time and at the end of the four days he'd see where matters stood. It shouldn't be so hard. He was accustomed to taking things as they came, wasn't he?

The hard part was going to be leaving her alone at night. How the hell was he going to be able to keep his hands off her for the next three nights? The brandy bottle hadn't done him much good last night.

It was finally old-fashioned willpower that he used that evening. It took more self-control than Judd had been forced to exercise for a long time but he managed to let Honor go off to bed alone after a quiet dinner and an even quieter evening sitting in front of the fireplace.

Then he sat by himself, gazing into the flames, and wondered why he had bothered to build the fire. It was really too warm for one. Somehow he'd thought it might seem romantic to Honor, though.

She'd seemed content to just sit curled like a cat in front of it, however, hardly saying a word the whole evening. Maybe fires weren't conducive to conversation. She'd talked plenty down in Mexico without the aid of a fire, he reminded himself. Maybe fires made her pensive and untalkative. Tomorrow night he'd have to try something else. He'd rather have her yelling at him than quiet and withdrawn as she had been tonight.

Why wasn't she asking him questions the way she

had during the evenings in Mexico? Why didn't she tell him about herself? How did you get a woman to talk to you? He'd never actually worried about the problem before, Judd knew. Women just sort of came and went in his life. He'd never thought much about trying to make one stay. In his mind he conjured up an image of the cozy conversation Honor had appeared to be having with her "friend" in Phoenix the previous evening. The guy in the three-piece suit hadn't seemed to have much trouble talking to Honor or getting her to talk to him.

Judd tried to remember if he had ever even owned a three-piece suit. If he had he couldn't recall it. His hand tightened around the brandy snifter. He wasn't going to rely on the brandy tonight, he told himself. He was simply having a nightcap. That was all.

The flames flickered and began to die on the hearth as he watched broodingly. What else had the guy in the three-piece suit done to get Honor to talk so readily? Inspiration dawned so suddenly, Judd blinked. Honor's "friend" had taken her out on a real date. He'd taken her to a cocktail lounge, danced with her and was probably planning to have dinner with her later. Then the "friend" undoubtedly had planned to take her home and make one hell of a heavy pass. Judd's eyes narrowed coldly as he followed the logic of the situation to its most likely conclusion. For a moment he felt like strangling the handsome "friend" in the three-piece suit.

There was no point torturing himself with thoughts of another man kissing Honor. Judd reminded himself that he had taken her away before anything like that could happen. Slowly he relaxed his fingers around the brandy snifter. He had to think about tomorrow, especially tomorrow evening. When it came to something as crucial as this he was not above taking lessons from a pro. If inviting Honor out on a real date was what worked for the guy in the three-piece suit, then Judd was willing to try it, too.

He broached the subject the next morning over breakfast, trying to keep it casual. He didn't dare let her know how desperate he was feeling. "I thought we could spend the day taking in some of Albuquerque. Maybe go to Old Town and the Indian Pueblo Cultural Center. Then, this evening there's a restaurant I know that has great steaks. Would you like that? It has a lounge and we can dance."

Honor looked up from her grapefruit. "Can you dance?"

Judd wondered if she was teasing him. Was that deliberate mischief in her eyes? He was not always able to tell. "I'm a little out of practice but I think I can get by," he told her roughly. He hoped. Out of practice was putting it mildly. He hadn't taken a woman out dancing in years. Judd looked down at his grapefruit and decided he really must be considered something of an outright bore by the female of the species.

"I think," Honor said from the other side of the table, "that sounds like a very nice idea. I'd like to go out for dinner and dancing this evening."

An incredible sensation of relief was Judd's first reaction. She was going to give him a chance after all. Now all he had to do was figure out how to get her back into her conversational mood, the one where she asked him questions and seemed genuinely interested in his life.

Fortunately the sightseeing in the restored Old

Town section of Albuquerque provided some stimulus for discussion, as did the Pueblo Cultural Center. Judd was exceedingly grateful for it.

"I've lived here for years and I hardly ever get down here," he remarked as they strolled through the shops and galleries of the restored area of the city. Albuquerque had been founded in 1706, and this part of town had been redone to re-create that early era. The Spanish colonial influence was rich and lasting.

"When did you move to Albuquerque?" Honor asked idly, stopping to examine a pottery vase filled with huge dried flowers.

Judd frowned behind her. Should he buy the vase and flowers for her? Did she really want them? Perhaps they were only of passing interest. "I came here about five years ago after I decided to set up the ferrying business."

"Where did you live before that?" she asked, going on to explore a row of kachina dolls.

Finally! She was starting to talk. Now all he had to do was keep up his end of the conversation. Should he offer to buy one of the kachina dolls? "Here and there." Hell, what kind of an answer was that? Desperately he tried to think of a more informative response. "I, uh, spent a lot of my time in South America before that. Technically I guess you could say I lived in Tucson. I used to keep an apartment there, at any rate." What now?

"Why did you spend so much time south of the border?" Honor picked up a small, carved wooden horse.

"I know my way around that part of the world and people used to hire me to fly stuff there. . . ." Judd's voice trailed off lamely as he tried to think of a way to explain the nomadic, rough-and-ready existence he'd led for so many years.

"What sort of stuff?"

He tried to think. Maybe she'd like the toy horse as a souvenir. Did women want souvenirs of a kidnapping? he asked himself wryly. "Medicine, supplies, food. Whatever. If the money was right, I'd fly it."

"Have you always been for sale, Judd?" she asked softly, lifting her eyes to meet his.

Sudden rage overwhelmed his good intentions. This woman could send him over the edge faster than anyone he had ever met in his life. "It's called working for a living, damn it!"

"You just made it a policy not to ask too many questions when you accepted a job, right?"

He fought down the tide of anger. If he exploded now he'd lose her. There would be nothing he could do to catch her here and carry her home. There was a cop not twenty feet away. All she had to do was start screaming. . . .

Judd reached out and yanked the toy horse out of her hand. As she stared at him in astonishment he turned on his heel and walked toward the nearest cashier. Wordlessly he paid for the toy and then he thrust the paper bag which now contained it into Honor's fingers. "Here. A souvenir. Let's go."

She trailed obediently after him as he led the way back to where he had parked the jeep. She walked right past the cop without so much as a murmur, but there was no more conversation to be had from her until they reached his home. Then all she said was, "What time are we going out tonight?"

"Six." He watched unhappily as she nodded and went to her room. It was two hours until six. Was she going to stay in there the whole time? At least down in Mexico that shack of hers had been too small to provide her any privacy. She had been forced to stay in the same room with him nearly all the time. With a sigh Judd went into his ōwn bedroom and pulled open the closet door. Somewhere, probably buried way in the back, he had a jacket and tie. Not a three-piece suit, but a jacket and tie that sort of went together after a fashion. Gloomily he began searching for them.

In her own room Honor stretched out the process of getting ready for the big date as long as possible. She took an extended bath instead of a shower, brushed her hair until it shone, and then she slowly put on the yellow dress she had been wearing the night Judd had abducted her. After trying a variety of knots and twists she elected to leave her hair loose around her shoulders. When she had finished she still had nearly forty-five minutes to kill until six o'clock.

It was no use. Unless she intended to spend the time sitting alone in her room, she was going to have to emerge and deal with Judd. Her eyes went to the paper bag containing the toy horse, and in spite of herself she smiled. Poor Judd. He wasn't accustomed to giving presents. Impulsively she opened the door and walked out into the living room.

He was standing at the window, staring out at the surrounding desert, a drink in his hand. For a long moment Honor just stared and then she smiled slowly. "I hardly recognized you."

He swung around, dark gaze taking in the picture she made in her vivid yellow-and-purple dress. She felt the heat of his eyes as if it were a palpable sensation, and a small, expectant shiver ran through her nerve endings. All this man had to do to kindle the longing was to look at her. She loved him. She had fallen for a ruthless mercenary who knew nothing of the gentle, sensitive side of life, a man who didn't know the meaning of unequivocal trust, who didn't believe in romanticizing the basic relationship between men and women. A man who didn't understand love. How could she have been so foolish?

How could she have prevented the inevitable, though? There were some things in life, Honor had learned during the past few weeks, over which a woman had little control. It was fate that had sent her to Garrison and Prager's office that night in Hong Kong and it was fate that had brought Judd Raven into Mexico searching for her. The whole chain of events was far too complex to unravel now. She was enmeshed in the net they had created, tied to the kind of man she would never even have met in the normal course of events.

She realized that this was the first time she had ever seen him dressed in anything besides black denims and dark shirts. This evening he actually had on a pair of slacks, a well-cut tan jacket and a muted tie. His dark hair was still damp from the shower and brushed back off his forehead. Honor experienced a strong urge to run her fingers through the carefully combed hair. Perhaps it was simply a strong urge to touch him, period.

"You're ready early," he said quietly, his eyes still resting on her slender figure.

"Yes."

He seemed vaguely uncertain for a moment and then he set down his drink with a restless movement. "Well, then, why don't we be on our way? We can have a sundowner drink at the restaurant before dinner."

Honor nodded, gaining the distinct impression he was anxious to get her out of the house. It was as if he didn't know quite what to do with her.

"I've put the top up on the jeep," he said as they walked outside, "so your hair won't get mussed."

"Thank you," she said politely, aware that his eyes were lingering now on her hair. She knew he wanted to reach out and touch it and wondered why he didn't do exactly that. The restlessness in him was unnerving. Judd always seemed so very sure of himself.

The restaurant he had chosen was warm and inviting. There was a pleasant intimacy about the rustic southwestern decor. The lounge was beginning to fill up with the cocktail crowd, but Judd managed to find a small corner table.

"I haven't been here in a long time," he began apologetically. "I hope the food is still good."

Good heavens! Now he was worrying about the food. Honor smiled a little distantly and sipped at the margarita he had ordered for her. What was the matter with Judd this evening? He acted as if he were trying to walk on eggshells. "I take it you don't get out much?" she hazarded dryly.

He gave her a sharp glance and then shrugged. "Does it show?"

"A little."

"I admit that taking a woman out on a real date doesn't come as naturally to me as it seemed to come to your friend in Phoenix," he muttered, looking down at his margarita. "I'm more at home in a sleazy Mexican cantina, I suppose."

"It wasn't a sleazy cantina! Everyone was very nice to me there," she protested, smiling.

He closed his eyes briefly as if counting to ten and then opened them to give her a very level stare. "You don't know how damn lucky you were to flit through that part of Mexico all by yourself without any major disasters."

"At the time I thought the only disaster that had befallen me was having you show up."

Judd studied her composed expression and she wondered if he could read anything at all in her face. She hoped not. He seemed to gather himself for the next question, as if he weren't sure he wanted to hear her answer.

"Do you still consider my arrival a disaster?"

She hesitated and then said smoothly, "It all worked out for the best in the end, didn't it? I'd still be down there, cowering every time a stranger showed up in the village, if it hadn't been for you." Judging by the brooding stare he gave her, that wasn't quite what he had wanted to hear.

"Honor, if I had it to do over again . . ." he began grimly and then let the sentence trail off into nothingness.

"Yes? If you had it to do over again, what would you do differently?" she prodded curiously.

He sighed. "Nothing. Given the same set of circumstances, I probably would behave in exactly the same way. I would have taken the job because it paid well and I would have wound up trying to sort out the truth of the situation in my own fashion instead of romantically declaring myself your unquestioning champion, right or wrong."

She sipped her drink. "Well, that's honest, at least."

"I've tried to be honest with you from the first."

"Yes, you have. You behaved very reasonably in Mexico, Judd. I was the one who was unreasonable." If he could be honest, so could she. "I read far too much into what happened between us that night. And you were perfectly right when you accused me of romanticizing the situation. I've always been something of a romantic, I guess. That was one of the reasons I came to Arizona."

"It was?" He appeared to want to say something else, something about her confession that she had been in the wrong, but Honor got the impression he didn't know how to phrase it.

"Ummm. I moved to the Southwest because I find the desert and the mountains spectacular. And I love the blend of cultures in this part of the country. I grew up in the Northeast, but for as long as I can remember there's been a certain pull about this part of the country."

"Your family? Do they still live in the Northeast?" he asked.

She hesitated and then nodded. "Oh, yes, they still live there. I don't see much of them," she admitted. "I didn't really fit in. That's an odd thing to say, isn't it? That you didn't fit into your own family?"

"Why didn't you?"

She lifted one shoulder uneasily. "Something to do with the whole lifestyle. My father is a banker and my mother is very *New England,* if you know what I mean. I always played with the right children, went to the right schools. I was quite a little preppy monster there for a time." She chuckled reminiscently. "But as

I grew older I grew more and more restless. I knew I wasn't going to marry the right man and become a community-conscious corporate wife. I began to feel trapped. So after I graduated from college I fled to the Southwest. My romantic escape!"

"You didn't go to your parents when you found yourself in trouble," Judd noted coolly.

Honor shook her head emphatically. "They would have thought I was a raving lunatic. Just as you did." He winced but she didn't bother to soothe his conscience. "In any event I couldn't deliberately bring Garrison and Prager down on them, could I? I had no right to put my parents in jeopardy."

There was a silence and then Judd said quietly, "You mean you didn't even feel close enough to your parents to be sure they would believe you?"

Honor bit her lip as she acknowledged his surprisingly accurate assessment of the situation. "No."

"My God," he breathed. "You're really on your own, aren't you? In spite of having a family."

"I suppose you could say that," she agreed slowly. "What about you, Judd? Do your parents know how you make your living?"

His mouth twisted in wry amusement. "My mother gave me up for adoption when I was two years old. I have no idea what she thinks about my career. Lord knows who my father was."

Honor's mood was suddenly softened by compassion. "Were you adopted, then?"

"I'm told I was a difficult child," he murmured dryly. "In any event I never seemed to last too long in the various homes where the agency tried to place me. No, I never got myself adopted. I guess I gave everyone a lot of trouble until I was fifteen. Then I discovered airports. I started hanging out around the field near town and conned a pilot into taking me up for a ride. After my first flight I knew what I was going to do with the rest of my life. As soon as I got my license I started taking any job that would keep me in airplane fuel."

"I guess I can see now why you never got married," Honor heard herself say wistfully. "What woman could compete with your love of flying?"

His voice hardened. "In spite of what you seem to think is some sort of unnatural relationship between me and my plane, I am capable of a few other interests in life!"

"Such as a good steak?" she challenged with a mischievous smile. "Or a glass of tequila?"

Belatedly he saw the laughter in her and answered with a crooked smile. "Exactly," he said very smoothly. "Shall we go into the restaurant and eat? I seem to have worked up an appetite."

"Is it such an effort to keep your fingers from going around my throat?"

He grinned, a slow, laughter-filled grin that reached his eyes. "You know me so well," he murmured, getting to his feet and taking her hand.

"They say you never really know a man until he's tried to teach you flying," she quipped.

"Who says that?"

"Oh, I don't know. Surely any number of women who have known pilots," she answered vaguely.

The mood for dinner seemed to have been established. Somehow the conversation began to flow more freely after that, enlivened by Honor's natural propensity to tease and Judd's equally natural tendency to react to her mockery.

The words began to come so easily to him that Judd found himself wondering how he could ever have been worried. Hell, it was obvious that under the right circumstances he was a fantastic conversationalist. Almost as good as the guy in the three-piece suit. The right circumstances, though, seemed to be limited to being with the right woman. It was only Honor to whom he could imagine himself talking so fluently. He found himself telling her about his first solo landing, the times he had flown into incredibly narrow jungle landing strips, the strange people he had worked for off and on through the years and a lot more that he had never told anyone else.

During the course of the evening his rampant curiosity about Honor led him, in turn, to ask one question after another. He learned more about the fierce independence that animated her, finding it an odd complement to the equally strong romantic side of her nature. She fascinated him, and at last he was beginning to understand some of the reasons why.

It was after dinner that he remembered he had promised her an opportunity to dance in the lounge. He had a pang of regret at the rashness of the offer but then recalled that it would give him a perfect chance to hold her in his arms for a while. That thought consoled him as he wondered if he was going to make a fool of himself on the floor. It had been so long. . . .

Honor went into his arms without any such concerns. Any man as coordinated and intrinsically grace-ful as Judd Raven would just naturally have to be a good dancer. She was right. He held her a little too close but other than that there was no real problem. She wasn't in a mood to try a lot of fancy steps anyway. The slow, romantic music was just what she wanted that night.

Judd's hand seemed to glide along the length of her spine, urging her closer with each step. Honor found herself relaxing against him, her head nestled on his shoulder and the warm, masculine scent of him filling her nostrils. Here on the floor, wrapped in his arms and the music, she found it was easy to forget the uneasy nature of their relationship. Why was it so simple to forget the past and the future whenever she found herself in Judd's arms? It must have something to do with the limited vision of love. Or perhaps it was just that love set its own priorities.

Conversation lagged again while they were dancing, but this time it was a comfortable silence. "Thinking about the Cessna?" she joked after a while. "Wondering if it's all tucked in for the night?"

"Actually I was thinking about what it would be like to tuck you in for the night," Judd retorted gently. His hand slipped to the curve of her hip and he felt the tiny shiver that went through her. Instantly his grip tightened until she was pressed close against the hard line of his thighs.

"But you're not going to find out, are you?" she asked, trying to keep her tone light and wicked. "I seem to recall a certain vow you made to keep your hands off me for the next couple of days. And we all know about your amazing self-control. . . . Oh!" She gasped as he came to a halt in the middle of the floor.

"You should know by now that you have the power to make me forget all about my self-control," he muttered thickly. His hands settled at her waist and he lowered his head to find her mouth.

She could feel the imprint his strong fingers were leaving on her skin and the room spun as he crushed her mouth with avid hunger. Around them the other dancers moved like shadows. Honor's arms crept up to circle Judd's neck and she sighed very softly.

Slowly he began to move them once more to the subtle beat of the music, his mouth lingering on hers. "Honor?"

"Ummm?" She stirred languidly in his grasp.

"I don't think I'm going to be able to live up to my promise tonight," he growled huskily against her cheek. His hands flexed at her waist as if he badly wanted to touch her bare skin. "Will you let me take you home and make love to you?"

"Do I have a choice?" she whispered, trembling a little at the urgency of his tone.

He hesitated and then said bluntly, "No, not if I can help it. God, I want you, woman. Please don't fight me." Judd lifted his head and stared down at her with glittering obsidian eyes that seemed to burn into her soul. "Let me take you home and make you mine. I'm going out of my head just thinking about the feel of you under me, the way you turn to flame when I touch you. I can't—"

"Judd, stop it!" she cried softly, her knees growing weak under the spell of his undoubted passion. "You mustn't talk like that. Not here on a dance floor, for heaven's sake!" But she knew he had already felt her reaction. How could she stop him tonight when she could feel the rising desire coursing through her veins? She was in love with this man. She would probably never be able to stop him from making love to her whenever he chose.

"Then let's get out of here," Judd said briskly, dropping his hands from her waist and taking her wrist. He started toward the door.

"Wait a minute! We're supposed to be on a date. You promised me dancing and a lovely evening and everything!" She tried unsuccessfully to free her fingers from his grasp but he had her out the door.

"You already know damn good and well I'm not the romantic type!" he growled as he pulled her toward the parked jeep.

"Then what type are you?" she demanded.

He spun around when he reached the jeep, his expression relentless and urgent. "Honor, don't play games with me tonight. I want you and I know you want me. I could feel you trembling back there on the dance floor. And surely to God you know what you do to me!"

She turned her face up, the moonlight making her look very pale in the velvet darkness. "You haven't answered my question, Judd," she said evenly. "What type of man are you?"

"I don't know what the hell you mean by that! You know exactly what type of man I am. I'm the same man I was when you pointed a gun at me that first night in Mexico. I'm the damned mercenary who accepted the contract to find you and bring you out of Mexico. Two thousand dollars plus expenses, remember? I'm the guy who spent the morning yelling at you in the cockpit of an airplane. I'm the man who kidnapped you from your home in Phoenix. I am not romantic. There are a few things in my past that won't stand up very well to close scrutiny. I don't always understand your sense of humor and your parents would probably collapse in shock if they ever met me.

But, by God, I want you, Honor Knight, and I'm going to do whatever I have to do to keep you. Is that very clear?"

Honor felt her soft, romantic mood slipping away in the face of his unexpected harshness. "Why are you yelling at me? We've had a lovely evening so far and now you're ruining it!"

"I'm trying to put things in perspective. I want you to know exactly where I stand. I'm sorry if I'm ruining the evening but I seem to make a habit of doing that, don't I? Entertaining a woman for an evening isn't my forte."

"But yanking her home and taking her to bed is? You're pretty fundamental in your outlook on life, aren't you, Judd? You just do as you damn well please. You fly your plane, make a few bucks now and then off jobs you don't question too thoroughly, drink a little tequila and occasionally, when it suits your mood, take a woman to bed."

He stared stonily down at her for a long instant. "You're trying to make me lose my temper, aren't you?" he finally asked. "Why, I wonder?"

"Maybe because when you lose your temper you seem almost human," she whispered throatily.

They stood searching each other's faces beneath the cold glare of the parking-lot light, and then Judd opened the door of the jeep and pushed her gently inside. "Come on, Honor. We're going home."

"To bed?" she demanded tightly.

"To talk. I think we need to talk a little more tonight." He got in beside her and started the engine. Without a word he pulled out of the parking lot and onto the street.

The drive to his home was one of the longest of

Honor's life. She alternated between hope and despair. Every time she thought she had made some progress toward reaching Judd on an emotional level things seemed to collapse. Right now she had no idea of the mood he was in. Was he angry? Was he still feeling passionate? It didn't matter, because he was back in full control of himself and during those times she felt locked out as solidly as if he had slammed a door in her face. It seemed to Honor that she had been trying to open that door ever since she had met him.

The house was dark, just as they had left it, and when Judd killed the engine Honor automatically reached for her own door handle. She was feeling increasingly nervous about what lay ahead, a part of her longing to resolve the tense situation between herself and the complex man she loved. But another part of her warned that she might not like the resolution. At least while things were uncertain there was hope.

As Judd reached for the keys in his pocket he realized his hand was shaking a little and the knowledge irritated him. Right now a lot of things irritated him. Everything had been going so perfectly. Why had he gone and ruined it all by dragging Honor off the dance floor? Was he never going to learn?

Maybe it was the pressure of that damned time limit she had given him. Four days. And he only had a couple left. They *had* to talk tonight. He had to make her understand that he couldn't just let her walk away from him.

Afterward, he decided it was because he was concentrating so hard on how to handle Honor that he failed to react to the situation inside the house until it was much too late. On the other hand, he told himself grimly, there wasn't a whole hell of a lot he could have done.

He simply hadn't been expecting to open the front door and find Nick Prager sitting in his living room holding a gun.

"Well, well, Mr. Raven. It's about time you got home. I've been waiting for you for two hours." Nick's cool gray eyes switched to Honor, who stood quite still beside Judd. "So now I know what happened to you, honey. I've been wondering."

"What the hell do you want with us?" Judd asked coldly.

"Isn't it obvious? I need someone to fly me over the border. I managed to slip into the country on a fake passport but I seem to be having a little trouble finding a way out. Then I remembered that you're always available for hire if the price is right, Mr. Raven. Believe me, tonight the price is going to be most attractive. Fifty thousand dollars for a few hours of your time. For that kind of money I'm sure you won't mind throwing Miss Knight into the bargain, will you? I have a small score to settle with her."

Chapter 11

"FIFTY THOUSAND?"

Honor heard Judd repeat the figure as he calmly turned and closed the door. Then he lounged back against it, his arms folded across his chest, midnight eyes focused on the handsome face of his uninvited visitor. Honor watched the two men as if she were a rabbit in the presence of two predators: a raven and a snake. She eyed Nick Prager's well-groomed brown hair, expensive business suit and smooth countenance, and wondered how she could ever have dated the snake. At least with the raven you knew right where you stood.

"You heard right, Raven. Fifty thousand." Nick smiled with chilling satisfaction. The hand holding the gun never wavered. "Interested?"

Judd didn't move. "You have the money on you?"

Nick patted a small suitcase standing beside the chair in which he was sitting. "Right here."

"How far into Mexico?"

"Some place I can catch a commercial jet liner," Nick said easily. "The Mexican authorities won't be on the lookout for me. Once I get back to Hong Kong I'll have no more problems. I have friends there. What do you say, Raven?" Nick waved the gun in a small arc, calling attention to it. Then he smiled again. "Shall we do business together?"

"I generally don't work well when I'm looking down the wrong end of a gun," Judd drawled.

"I understand, but you see I'm a little nervous lately. Ever since my partner experienced a problem tying up some loose ends, I've felt more comfortable carrying this unpleasant piece of metal. Tell me, what did go wrong on the assignment we gave you, Judd?" Nick glanced at Honor in mild disgust. "Did the little bitch offer you more than we did? Or did you find her so good in bed you couldn't bear to give her up to Leo? I always wondered what she would be like in the sack. I had intended to find out in Hong Kong but things didn't quite work out, did they, Honor? Leo and I knew you'd flown home to Phoenix, but it took us a while to find out that you'd slipped over the border into Mexico."

"But when you did you went right out and hired Judd to find me, didn't you? That was quite a story you gave him, Nick, about being my brother. Leo played the distraught father, I gather."

"The tale was a little weak in places but we understood from our sources that it wasn't Mr. Raven's practice to ask too many questions if the price was right. I had to return to Hong Kong to finish some business there, so after we lined Raven up I left the country." Nick swung his sardonic gaze back to the quiet man leaning against the door. "You should have told us that we weren't offering enough, Raven. Leo and I would have been willing to pay much more for Honor."

"You offered enough. I did what I was paid to do. I brought her out of Mexico. It was at Garrison's end that things went wrong. The Feds got him before I could complete the contract."

"And just how did the Feds get onto Leo?" Nick mused icily. "Were they the ones who made the better offer? Are you playing both sides of the street, Raven?"

"It's not too profitable these days," Judd murmured dryly. "What with Federal budget cutbacks, government contracts just don't pay like they once did."

"Then what the hell went wrong, Raven? Why was Leo picked up? Why did my connections warn me about using my real passport to get into the country? Come on, don't tell me you and Honor didn't have a hand in that somewhere!"

"The information I got was that the Feds have been watching you and Garrison for some time. They closed in at about the same time I was bringing Honor out of Mexico."

"Quite a coincidence." Nick shot a scathing glance at Honor's tense face. "So why did you hang on to Miss Knight? Just trying to salvage something from an otherwise busted deal?"

Honor took her courage in both hands, making a desperate effort to keep her voice as cool as that of the predators in the room. "When Garrison wasn't able to pay off, Mr. Raven suddenly found himself open to other offers. I made him a good one."

"Really?" Nick eyed her skeptically. "What are you paying him for?"

"Isn't it obvious? To protect me from you. I knew you'd be coming after me eventually, Nick."

"Mr. Raven, it seems, has had a lot of business lately."

"But not much in the way of cold cash," Judd interposed flatly. "The economy being what it is these days, I've decided on a general policy of getting the money up front. I'm sure, being a businessman yourself, you can understand my reasoning."

Nick used the toe of his shoe to nudge the suitcase around where he could reach it with his free hand. Without taking his eyes off Judd and keeping the gun unwaveringly pointed at him, Nick leaned over and flipped open the locks. When he raised the lid of the case several neatly bound bundles of currency came into view. "Up-front money, Mr. Raven. Far more than Miss Knight could possibly afford. When I got news of Leo's arrest I came back to close out the company's U.S. bank account. It's all in cash, and fifty thousand of it is yours. How soon can we leave for Mexico?"

Honor held her breath, watching Judd's eyes go briefly to the stacks of money and then lift to meet Nick's waiting gaze. "Just as soon as you like, Prager. For that kind of cash I'm always at your service," he said softly.

Nick nodded grimly. "I had a hunch that might be the case."

"But I still don't like working with a gun at my head."

"I can't blame you, but you must see that I've got to be a bit cautious. I'm in a somewhat precarious position as long as I'm on this side of the border. I'm afraid I'll have to hang on to the gun for a while."

"And the money?" Judd glanced at the suitcase as Nick closed and locked it.

"It will be with us in the plane. I shall leave your share behind when I get out in Mexico. At that point I will also take Miss Knight off your hands. You're probably growing tired of her by now anyway, hmmm?"

Honor felt a chill race down her spine as she glanced at Judd's impassive face. But he said nothing, merely pushed himself away from the door. He didn't look at Honor as he reached around to open it again. "Let's go. It's getting late."

"Excellent, Raven. I'm in something of a hurry myself." Prager got to his feet and picked up the suitcase. Then he motioned with the gun. "Come along, Honor. I know you're an incurable romantic but you're going to have to accept a few facts of life. One of them is that to someone like Mr. Raven fifty grand is going to speak a lot louder than a toss in the hay. Move."

Unwillingly Honor's gaze dropped to the suitcase in the gunman's hand. Fifty thousand dollars. She wondered how often in his career Judd had received an offer of that magnitude. Probably seldom. She swallowed awkwardly and then turned toward the door. Judd stood waiting, his expression as emotionless and unreadable as it had ever been. His gaze slid away from her as he pulled a set of keys out of his pocket.

"I have a rental car parked at the back of the house," Nick said calmly as he shepherded the other two outside. "Might as well leave it there since the jeep is handier. You sit in front beside Raven, Honor. I'll get in the back so that I can keep an eye on both of you."

The drive to the deserted airfield was made in taut silence. The whistling of the night wind through the open window was the only sound. When they reached the field Judd parked the jeep near the old hangar. In the moonlight the row of small private planes stood like a pack of night creatures on the tarmac.

"I'll have to turn on the runway lights." Judd was already striding toward the tiny office housed at the entrance of the hangar.

"All right. Follow him, Honor. Stay where I can keep track of both of you or I won't wait until we reach Mexico before I settle my score with you." Prager motioned once more with the gun.

Honor shivered as moonlight glanced along the black metallic barrel of the weapon and then obediently turned to follow Judd. At the entrance to the office she watched in silence as Judd flipped a switch. Out on the runway two long rows of lights blinked into existence.

"Will the lights attract attention at this time of night?" Prager demanded uneasily.

Judd shook his head once. "No. If anyone notices he'll just assume someone's practicing a little night flying. Happens all the time. Are you ready?"

"I'm ready. Honor will ride in front with you again, I think. I'll take the backseat."

Judd nodded, saying nothing, and started out to the waiting Cessna. Honor trailed along behind him, terrifyingly aware of the gun pointed at her back. Her fingers were already beginning to tremble, she realized distantly. Nervously she watched Judd go through his preflight check and then Prager was ordering her into the plane.

Ten minutes later, with Prager still holding his gun and sitting behind Honor, Judd lifted the Cessna off the runway into the night sky over Albuquerque. He shot a quick glance at Honor's stark expression and then concentrated on his flying. There was nothing he could say or do to soothe her now. She'd been through a hell of a lot because of that bastard in the backseat and there was more to come before the night was over. One gutsy lady.

He let the plane climb rapidly, seeking plenty of altitude. The field elevation was a little over five thousand feet which meant he needed a bit above ten. He watched the needle slip past the numbers on the altimeter, seventy-five hundred, eight thousand. . . .

What was Honor thinking? Was she remembering the sight of all that money in the suitcase and wondering how much fifty thousand would mean to a mercenary who never asked too many questions about the jobs he accepted? Eighty-five hundred feet. Nine thousand.

She was frightened but she was in control, he realized. Just as she had been in control of her fear that night when he'd found her in the cantina in Mexico. He remembered his own feelings that night as he had stared at her through the smoke of the noisy cantina. After a week of looking he'd finally found the woman in the photograph and the reality was even more intriguing than the image. She'd been scared but defiant and she'd kept her head, trying to bribe him and then, later, trying to use the gun.

He'd never forget listening to her slowly remove the cheap weapon from the bedside drawer. After he'd found the bullets he'd been curious to see whether or not she'd have the nerve to try the gun. And then he recalled the way she had hurled herself at him in frustrated fury and the way she had felt beneath him when he'd finally succeeded in subduing her. It had required all his willpower not to take her that night. He'd wanted her so badly.

The altimeter needle passed ninety-five hundred feet. Other images flashed in Judd's mind, memories of the way Honor had taunted him that day beside the stream until he had finally realized she was playing with him; memories of the way she had responded to him in bed.

And now she sat beside him wondering if he was going to wind up being her executioner after all. Ninety-nine hundred feet . . .

Quite suddenly Judd realized exactly how Honor must have felt the morning after he had first made love to her. He knew because right now he wanted her to have complete faith in him. Just as she had wanted him to have complete trust in her that morning. He didn't want her waiting to see if he'd take the money. He didn't want her wondering whether fifty thousand dollars meant more than having her in his bed. He didn't want her to take a wait-and-see attitude while the logic of the situation developed.

He wanted complete, unequivocal trust from her. Judd's hands tightened on the wheel.

Out of the corner of his eye he saw moonlight glint

off the gun barrel in Prager's hand. The altimeter needle passed through ten thousand. Ten thousand should be enough. He eased back on the throttle and slowly brought up the Cessna's nose. The little plane began to slow. He applied more back pressure on the wheel and the Cessna began to fight him, seeking a level attitude.

Honor glanced at him and he saw her grip the edge of her seat. Did she realize what was happening? There was no time to wonder what was going through her head now. Judd eased the wheel back farther and the airspeed fell off drastically as the nose of the plane climbed past the horizon.

"Hey, what the hell's going on?" Finally Nick Prager began to realize something was wrong.

Judd felt the shudder that preceded the stall. An instant later the stall took hold.

"Raven! Damn it, what's happening?" There was an element of panic in Prager's voice as the Cessna stalled. *"What's wrong?"*

Judd kicked in the right rudder and the plane turned almost lazily into a right spin as the nose dropped sickeningly downward. Prager yelled as a split second later the sprinkling of lights on the desert floor began to whirl dizzily beneath them. The Cessna spun violently toward the ground.

"Raven!" Prager's tone was now filled with panic. "Raven, stop it!"

Honor said nothing. She clutched the edges of her seat and sat staring stonily through the windshield as the plane spun downward.

Raven watched his instruments, counting spins and altitude. "Hand the gun over to Honor, Prager. I told you I don't do my best work when I've got a weapon pointed at my head."

"Damn you! What the hell kind of game are you playing?" Prager screamed in violent fear. "I'll kill you both!"

"In that case there's no real incentive for me to bring this plane out of the spin, is there?"

"Raven! Listen to me! Fifty thousand dollars, man. I'll make it a hundred thousand!"

"I'll listen to the money, but not to the gun. Hand it to Honor."

The plane went through another revolution and the lights below swung around in a way that was bound to make anyone's stomach churn. Judd saw Honor unclench one of her hands and extend it back toward Prager.

"The gun, Nick," she gritted. "Give me the gun or he'll send us all into the ground. Believe me, he's a lot better at playing chicken than you are."

"Hand over the gun and then we'll talk about the money I'm going to get for this little assignment," Judd said calmly. He didn't have a whole lot more time. The ground was approaching at a terrifying rate.

"All right! All right, she's got the gun, now stop this crazy game!" Prager slapped the ugly weapon into Honor's hand and her fingers closed convulsively around it.

"You have it, Honor?" Judd didn't look at her. His eyes were on the instruments.

"I've got it," she whispered tightly.

"Okay, hang on."

As gently as possible Judd eased off on the back pressure he had been applying to the wheel and added opposite rudder. The Cessna obediently neutralized itself. The sickening spin halted. Now the plane was simply plunging headfirst toward the desert floor without the added effects of the spinning.

"Raven!" Prager was screaming as it became obvious they were in a headlong dive.

Honor didn't say a word. Slowly Judd eased the craft out of the dive, bringing the nose up very gently. No sense ruining things now by doing this part too fast and pulling off the wings! The effects of gravity asserted themselves as the plane came up out of the dive. Judd felt the familiar G forces sucking him down into his seat and wished he'd had time to tell Honor what to expect. She must be absolutely terrified by this point. Prager certainly was.

"My God, Raven," Nick Prager whispered from the backseat as the Cessna leveled off. "You're a bastard. A real, cold bastard. I wasn't going to cheat you out of the money. I fully intended to hand over the fifty thousand." His eyes slitted as he watched Honor turn in her seat and point his gun at him. "And I'll still make it a hundred thousand if you'll take another contract out on Miss Knight here."

"Another contract?" Judd asked, checking for nighttime landmarks on the desert below. The lights of the airfield should be coming up at about one o'clock.

"This time I want her dead," Prager hissed.

"Oh, for heaven's sake, Nick, don't sound so melodramatic." Honor smiled. "And don't waste your breath. Judd isn't going to take your fifty thousand to fly you into Mexico. He doesn't do that sort of work anymore. And he's not going to take the extra fifty for killing me, either. He's in love with me."

She saw the thunderstruck expression on Judd's face as he shot her a startled glance but Honor kept her attention on Prager. The gun in her hand was as unwavering as it had been when he held it. In that moment she didn't think it would bother her at all to use it.

"In love with you!" Prager spat violently. "Don't be such a dumb little bitch. Judd Raven will do anything if the money's right!"

"Not quite," Honor said gently. "You really don't know him very well, do you?"

"I know his reputation!"

"Which is somewhat exaggerated, I'm afraid." Honor chuckled. "He's got business ethics, you see. Scruples. You wouldn't understand about that sort of thing, Nick. But I'm afraid you're going to have to accept the fact that there are some things Judd Raven won't do for money."

Prager shot her a fulminating look and then pinned his desperate glance on Judd's set profile. "All right, so don't kill her if she's that good in bed. You can have the full hundred grand for the trip to Mexico."

"Forget it, Nick." Honor sighed. "Judd's not a true mercenary. I can't imagine why so many people have the wrong idea about him."

Judd cleared his throat, started to say something, broke off and then tried again just as he brought the Cessna into the downwind leg of a landing pattern. "I expect," he finally managed in a very soft voice, "it's because most people aren't close to me. They don't know me as well as you do."

"That must be it," Honor replied cheerfully. "But, then, I'm in love with you and that makes a difference."

Judd gave his full concentration to his landing. It was one of the most difficult of his life for some odd reason. Strange. He'd done plenty of night landings under far worse circumstances.

"What are we going to do with Prager?" Honor inquired conversationally as the Cessna rolled to a halt.

"We're going to phone Maddock and ask what he wants done with him," Judd replied tersely, unlatching the Cessna door.

He made the phone call, remembering to reverse the charges, and found Maddock at home.

"You've got him in Albuquerque?" Craig Maddock demanded, plainly astonished. "We knew he snuck past us getting into the country but we lost track of him two days ago."

"He wanted to be flown into Mexico," Judd explained. "Seemed to think I'd do the job."

He could almost see Maddock's eyebrows climb skyward. "And you weren't interested?"

"I've, uh, got a new business partner," Judd drawled, his eyes seeking Honor's face. "She vets my jobs these days. She decided we wouldn't take this one."

"I see." Maddock chuckled on the other end. "Well, I'll get someone to take him off your hands before you change your mind. There's a man in the Albuquerque office I can call. Where are you now?" Judd told him. "Okay, stay where you are. We'll have someone out there as soon as possible. Oh, and Judd . . ."

"Yeah?"

"Watch yourself. Prager's as nasty as they come."

"I didn't know you cared."

"It's not you I'm worrying about," Maddock growled. "It's your new business partner. She seems to be a good influence on you." He hung up the phone before Judd could slam his receiver down.

"What now?" Honor asked brightly. She had turned the gun over to Judd, who was keeping it idly trained on a sullen Prager.

"Now we wait. Maddock's sending someone to pick him up."

Honor seated herself on the old metal desk and swung her feet gently. She didn't look at Judd. "What an interesting evening this turned out to be."

"Didn't it, though?" he murmured. "Fascinating."

And once again Honor couldn't tell a thing about what he was thinking. They spent much of the waiting period in silence, neither one of them making any real effort to break it. Of course, Honor assured herself, Nick Prager's presence made it difficult to conduct a private conversation.

Still, by the time the Albuquerque authorities had come to collect Nick, Honor was beginning to feel slightly apprehensive. Judd hadn't spoken at all in the past twenty minutes and he seemed relieved when the official car arrived outside the hangar.

"Come on, Prager, your ride's here. The destination won't be Mexico, but that's the breaks. On your feet."

Honor waited quietly while the exchange was made. The two government men from the Albuquerque office were cool and competent. Judd talked to them in low tones for a few minutes and then, before Honor was quite ready, the car drove off with Prager and his new escorts. She was alone with Judd.

He came slowly back into the small office, his dark

eyes finding her instantly as he paused in the doorway. She thought he was looking at her very much the way he had looked at her that first night in the cantina. And she felt once again that atavistic chill that warned of the presence of the hunter.

For a long moment they stared at each other in utter silence. Then Judd asked quietly, "Were you frightened when I put the Cessna into a spin? There wasn't time to warn you."

"It's quite a dramatic maneuver, isn't it?" she murmured dryly. "Actually, all things considered, you're probably lucky I didn't throw up all over your precious plane."

His face softened. "I would have forgiven you under the circumstances."

Her mouth curved softly. "That would have been very understanding of you."

"I'll be willing to forgive you just about anything if you'll repeat what you said in the plane." He was watching her so intently Honor found herself gripping the edge of the desk.

"About not being a true mercenary?" she whispered. "You're not, you know. I've known that from the beginning. A real dyed-in-the-wool mercenary type would have handed me over to Garrison without a qualm. A genuine mercenary wouldn't have given me those four extra days in Mexico. And don't forget, I knew from the first that you had some ethics. Remember how you turned down my bribe?"

"That wasn't all you said in the Cessna," he reminded her slowly. "You said something about loving me."

"Oh, that." Her smile widened and her green-and-gold eyes were filled with gentleness.

"Yes, that. Honor, did you mean it?" he rasped. He didn't move from his position in the doorway. Every line of his body was taut and poised as if he were about to take wing.

"I meant it."

He stared at her. "Honor, I didn't . . . I wasn't what you wanted me to be that first morning after we went to bed together. I didn't give you the complete trust and faith that you wanted; that you *deserved*."

"No. You gave me your protection, instead. Have you ever looked after someone the way you looked after me, Judd?" she asked whimsically.

He shook his head, saying nothing. His silence was eloquent enough.

Honor slid off the desk and took a step toward him. "You didn't know anything at all about love so it's understandable."

"What's understandable?"

"That you didn't recognize the first signs of it in yourself." She took another step. "Offering me your protection was equivalent to another man's profession of undying love and devotion. It was my fault that I didn't realize it at the time. I suppose it's because I was so upset and frightened. I *had* romanticized that night, Judd. But I had no right to assume you would do the same. What I should have seen was the evidence of how much our night together had meant to you, too. I should have understood that by the way you handled things the next morning. You were intent on taking care of me."

"You hated me the next morning when I didn't react the way you wanted me to react," he got out savagely. His dark eyes were glittering with the violence of the feelings he was holding in check. He lifted a hand as Honor came a step nearer. Then he appeared to realize it was shaking a little and he lowered it quickly. "Honor, you were so warm and sweet and giving that night. All I did was take."

She shook her head. "No, Judd. You gave, too, but I was too wrapped up in my own hurt and disappointment the next morning to acknowledge it. You kept saying I belonged to you."

He winced. "I didn't phrase that very well, did I?"

"It was properly phrased. For you." Honor smiled again. "It just wasn't quite the attitude I had been expecting. Now I know that you were reaching out to me in the only way you could. The only way you knew how to reach out to a woman. Have you ever told another woman she belonged to you?"

"No. I never wanted another woman the way I want you," he returned starkly.

"You see? It was your instinctive way of extending another bond between us, but I was a little slow in seeing it. You were determined to protect me, to claim me and I should have realized how much that meant."

"When did you realize it?" This time Judd managed to get his hands to the level of Honor's shoulders. His fingers still shook a little but he had them more or less under control as he slid his palms up under her hair to cup her face.

"There was no blinding moment of understanding," she admitted. "I suppose Nick's total misconception of you did serve to put it all in perspective tonight, though. It amazed me that he actually thought you'd take his money to kill me."

"You knew I'd do no such thing?"

"Of course I knew that." She touched his hands

with her own as she stood looking up at him. Her eyes were brimming with her love. "We're very close, remember? And we're growing closer each day. Someday, Judd Raven, you're going to wake up and realize you're in love with me."

"Oh, God, Honor!" He pulled her nearer and some of the emotion that had been swirling in his dark eyes began to seep out in the form of tears. When Honor touched them with wondering fingertips he groaned and wrapped her fiercely against him. "Sweetheart, I'm a little slow, but I'm not *that* slow. You don't have to wait for me to come to some grand realization. I know damn good and well that I'm in love with you. Nothing else could explain the way I feel. *Nothing!* I ache, honey. I can't even bear to think of losing you. I would never have been able to let you go when the four days you gave me ran out."

"Judd, darling, please don't cry," she breathed shakily.

"Why not? I've tried a lot of other emotions out on you. You've made me laugh and you've made me lose my temper and you've made me hunger for you with a passion I've never known before. Why shouldn't I try a few tears?"

"Oh, Judd!"

"I love you, Honor. I love you, I love you, I love you!" He buried his face in her hair, dampening her cheek with his tears and repeated the words in wonder.

"You couldn't love me any more than I love you, darling Judd." And then Honor's tears were mingling with his own.

They held each other for a long, long time and then Judd took Honor home to bed. There was silence between them during the drive but this time there was understanding underlying the silence.

"This has been the longest night of my life," Judd whispered as he gathered Honor close in the four-poster bed an hour later. "I've never given a damn whether or not someone trusted me or believed in me before this evening. When I realized that was what I wanted from you I finally understood what you meant that morning in Mexico."

Honor reached up for him, her eyes soft with love. "No more talking, darling. Just love me."

"Maybe you're right," he murmured deeply. "Verbal communication doesn't seem to be one of my strong points."

"I wouldn't say that. You're getting better every day," Honor teased. "I think you have the talent, you just didn't get much practice with the Cessna!"

Chapter 12

LESS THAN A WEEK LATER HONOR WOKE UP TO FIND herself again in bed and again in Mexico. She leaned back against the pillows and surveyed the luxurious resort-hotel suite. This was no shack in a poor village. It was an elegant hotel on the tip of Baja. And she was a married woman on her honeymoon. Judd had been very insistent on marriage.

"I'm not going to spend the rest of my life being accused of kidnapping," he had declared forcefully.

"But, darling, you're so good at it," Honor had replied blithely. "Oh, well, at least this will give me a certain status over your plane, won't it? I mean, you can't *marry* an airplane under the laws of the state of New Mexico."

"I wonder if New Mexico ever got around to outlawing wife-beating?" Judd had mused.

Honor was remembering that remark when the door to the bathroom opened and her husband emerged wearing only a towel rather carelessly knotted around his lean hips. "What are you laughing at?" he demanded. His eyes moved over her as he crossed the room to sit down beside her on the bed.

"Your interest in the wife-beating laws of New Mexico."

"Oh, yes, I must remember to check on them when we get back. Being a husband does entail certain responsibilities." He leaned over her with mocking menace, imprisoning her slender body between his hands.

Honor blinked and then decided that it was, indeed, *mock* menace. Judd was still learning about things like play and the kind of teasing that went on between lovers. There were occasions, however, when Honor found that playing games with a bird of prey could still be a slightly uncertain business. "Ah, well, I suppose it adds spice," she murmured half to herself.

"What does?" He leaned closer, apparently fascinated with her mouth.

"Never knowing for sure if you're playing or if you're quite serious." She chuckled. "You can be rather intimidating, Judd."

"But you're not afraid of me, are you?" he asked in satisfaction. He trailed one finger down the line of her throat to where the hem of the sheet covered her breasts. "I've never wanted you to be afraid of me. I didn't like the look in your eyes that first night when I found you in the cantina. I'd been looking for you a solid week, pretending to everyone I met that you were my runaway wife. When I finally found you I had this idiotic notion that you did somehow belong to me. And I didn't want you afraid of me."

He leaned down and kissed her lingeringly, letting his fingers slide beneath the hem of the sheet as he did so. Slowly, tantalizingly he let his hand wander farther as he lazily explored her mouth with his own.

Honor stirred beneath the deepening caress. "Judd?"

"Hmmm?" He slowly began to lower the sheet.

"You don't mind having a . . . a business partner?"

"From all accounts you've got a terrific head for business. I'm looking forward to having you for a business partner." He began to nibble the side of her throat. "The clients are going to love you."

"You realize I won't be letting you accept any more questionable jobs from people like Craig Maddock or Garrison and Prager?" Honor began to thread her fingers through the raven-dark depths of his hair. Her body began to feel warm and receptive.

"There's not a lot of money in running a ferrying operation or doing charter work," he warned absently. He tugged the sheet down below her breasts and found the hardening peak of one nipple with his palm.

"We'll build up the business," she told him confidently. "In a few years we'll have other pilots working for us and we'll have a solid reputation."

"Whatever you say." He smiled as he felt her breast tighten under his touch. His dark eyes lit with a lambent flame.

"And if that doesn't work I can always get a job in Albuquerque," Honor said hastily.

He chuckled softly. "Things aren't going to get that bad. The ferrying business turns a steady profit. If we add a few more pilots to the staff we can keep ourselves in food and tequila. And you and I will have plenty of time to play," he added, sounding pleased.

"You're getting pretty good at that." She sighed blissfully. "Is tomorrow the day we fly over to the village and give everyone a ride in the Cessna?"

"Is that all right with you?"

"Oh, yes. I'm looking forward to seeing our old haunts again. So romantic, don't you think? You can buy me a drink in the cantina and we can spend the night in that little cottage."

"Ummm. But this time I won't be sleeping on the damned floor!"

"And I won't be trying to pull a gun on you in the middle of the night. Do you think we'll be bored?" Honor laughed softly.

Judd grinned. "Boredom has not been a big factor in my life since I met you." He reached out and deliberately pulled the sheet all the way down to her ankles. "You seem to have forgotten to put on your nightgown," he observed blandly.

"So I did. Shall I go and get it?"

"Don't you dare move," he drawled. His hand flattened on her stomach and slid lazily down to her thigh.

Honor felt the rising tension in him and knew it was mirrored in herself. "I love you, Judd," she whispered. The humor faded from her eyes to be replaced by passion.

"You couldn't love me any more than I love you." The laughter had left his dark eyes, too, and she could read the desire that took its place.

"I used to spend a lot of time wondering what you were thinking," she confided, running her hands in small, intimate circles across his bare shoulders.

"And now you seem to be able to read my mind."

"We've become very close," she said simply.

"I like being close to you, Honor Knight Raven." He slipped off his towel and stretched out beside her. "I've never experienced anything else like it in the whole world." He reached out and pulled her toward him, his hand curving lovingly around her hips. Then Judd took her mouth once more, his arm extending behind her head.

Honor moaned as the fires began to burn in her blood. Her fingers splayed against his chest and her legs flexed to curve between his. "Judd, oh, *Judd!*" She moved her hand down the broad planes of his chest to the hard line of his thigh and then she pushed at him gently, urging him over onto his back.

Judd fell against the pillows willingly, a warmly passionate smile edging his mouth as Honor leaned over him. "Ah, sweetheart, you make me feel so alive," he breathed as she began to rain tiny kisses down the length of his body. He pushed his fingers through her hair, delighting in the texture of it as she gently made love to him. "Alive and happy. That's how you make me feel, honey."

She gloried in the response of his body, delighting in the surging strength of his manhood as he stirred beneath her touch. The feel of his hair-roughened skin made her moan softly. Her teeth sank tantalizingly into his thigh.

"Take me, Honor," he growled, his hands going to her waist. "Come here and *take me*. You're driving me wild." He lifted her effortlessly, settling her astride his hips.

Honor felt his hands moving on her as she knelt above him and she knew a restless, hungry urge to make Judd lose control completely. She loved it when he seemed to be unable to withstand the temptation of her. Eagerly she sought to tease and torment him until he groaned beneath her. Hands fluttering lightly over his skin she set a heady rhythm with her body, one he was obliged to follow.

"You're a witch," he muttered huskily, midnight eyes flaming darkly. "You know I can't resist you."

"No?" She smiled down at him with dreamy wickedness.

"Are you going to tease me all night long?"

"Yes, I think so. I like teasing you."

"You have since the beginning, haven't you?" he accused thickly.

"You respond so well to teasing," she murmured and deliberately ran her fingers through the curling hair on his chest. Beneath her his hips arched upward, trying to force the pace of the slow lovemaking. But Honor stayed firmly in control.

"Sweetheart, put me out of my torment." He reached up to pull her closer but still she resisted. "My God, I want you so!"

"This is a new game I just invented." Honor slowed the pace still further, well aware of his mounting frustration.

"Raven-baiting?" he mocked heavily. "Don't you know I always win when we play games?" He twisted beneath her.

"Judd! No, wait!" But it was too late. Honor found herself flat on her back being crushed deeply into the bedding as Judd stretched out along the length of her. His gentle aggression sent a thrilling excitement through her and she was helpless to halt the loving assault.

"Part your lips for me, honey," he ordered roughly as he lowered his head.

Wordlessly she obeyed, loving the taste of him. Her arms wrapped around the bold contours of his back and she sighed into his throat.

"Now part your legs for me," he growled.

She felt the fierce surge of satisfaction and anticipation in him as she again obeyed. He came into her with a passionate ferocity that made the breath catch in her chest for an instant. Then she was caught up in the swift, spiraling climb to the heights.

There was no other bird that could master a raven in the air, she remembered dimly. And she was held tightly in her raven's talons. Faster and faster they flew until the warm lightning caught them both. Then they clung together through the slow, languorous descent. All the way to the ground Honor heard her name on Judd's lips. It was spoken with reverence and love and happiness and sheer, masculine possession.

Honor's eyes flickered open to find Judd propped on his elbow beside her, gazing down at her love-softened body. There was deep contentment and a trace of loving amusement in the hard lines of his face. His fingers idly stroked the scar on the inside of her wrist.

"Honor," he vowed huskily, "I'm going to do my best to make you happy. I know things started off badly between us and I know I'm not the kind of man you always dreamed of falling in love with but I'll—"

She put up a hand, covering his mouth and stopping the words. Her eyes smiled lovingly. "Are you worried about not being romantic enough for me?"

He nodded mutely.

She grinned. "Don't you know how marvelously

romantic it is for a woman to be abducted by the man she loves?"

He looked taken aback. "It is?"

"Definitely. We'll have to do it every other year on our anniversary."

"That sounds like an interesting sort of game," he decided, his eyes full of laughter.

"One you should excel at. You're a born hunter. A bird of prey."

"Ummm, maybe, but I think I prefer what happens after I get my hands on you to the hunt itself. Making love to you is a much more enjoyable pastime than hunting you down."

Judd leaned over and emphasized his words with a slow, possessive kiss and Honor gave herself up in complete trust to the embrace of the raven she had gentled.

Coming in October 1983
Janet Dailey

CALDER BORN CALDER BRED

The Calder family story which began so dramatically in <u>This Calder Sky</u> and continued in <u>This Calder Range</u> and <u>Stands A Calder Man</u> now comes to a close in this all-new novel, as powerful, as enthralling as the first three.

If you've thrilled to the first three Calder novels, you will not want to miss Janet Dailey's new novel—on sale in October.

....

Or, use the coupon below to order by mail
Pocket Books, Department 983
1230 Avenue of the Americas, New York, NY 10020
Please send me _____ copies of CALDER BORN, CALDER BRED (83610-2 / $6.95). Please add 75¢ to cover postage and handling. NYS and NYC residents please add appropriate sales tax. Send check or money order—no cash, stamps, or CODs, please. Allow six weeks for delivery.

Name_____

Address_____

City_____ State / ZIP_____

Silhouette Intimate Moments

Available Now

Raven's Prey by Stephanie James

Honor Knight had to convince Judd Raven the two men who
had hired him to find her weren't her father and brother.
Only Honor hadn't realized Judd was holding her prisoner
for his own reason: he was in love.

Against The Rules by Linda Howard

At seventeen Cathryn Ashe had fought Rule Jackson and lost.
Now, more sure of herself and her new-found independence,
she was ready to challenge him again—only this time,
her heart was at stake.

The Fires Of Winter by Beverly Bird

As editor of a small paper, Heather Cavelle tried to write only
of the good in the world. Then David Sullivan took over and
plunged the paper into a search for crime and hidden truths,
and what they discovered was their love for each other.

Fantasies by Pamela Wallace

When Spencer Tait met the new studio president
Devon O'Neill they clashed immediately. Tensions were high
and the future at stake as the cameras rolled—because this
time, the real story was taking place behind the scenes.

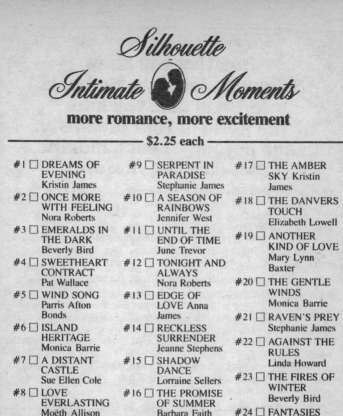

Silhouette
Intimate Moments

more romance, more excitement

———————— **$2.25 each** ————————

#1 ☐ DREAMS OF EVENING
Kristin James

#2 ☐ ONCE MORE WITH FEELING
Nora Roberts

#3 ☐ EMERALDS IN THE DARK
Beverly Bird

#4 ☐ SWEETHEART CONTRACT
Pat Wallace

#5 ☐ WIND SONG
Parris Afton Bonds

#6 ☐ ISLAND HERITAGE
Monica Barrie

#7 ☐ A DISTANT CASTLE
Sue Ellen Cole

#8 ☐ LOVE EVERLASTING
Moëth Allison

#9 ☐ SERPENT IN PARADISE
Stephanie James

#10 ☐ A SEASON OF RAINBOWS
Jennifer West

#11 ☐ UNTIL THE END OF TIME
June Trevor

#12 ☐ TONIGHT AND ALWAYS
Nora Roberts

#13 ☐ EDGE OF LOVE Anna James

#14 ☐ RECKLESS SURRENDER
Jeanne Stephens

#15 ☐ SHADOW DANCE
Lorraine Sellers

#16 ☐ THE PROMISE OF SUMMER
Barbara Faith

#17 ☐ THE AMBER SKY Kristin James

#18 ☐ THE DANVERS TOUCH
Elizabeth Lowell

#19 ☐ ANOTHER KIND OF LOVE
Mary Lynn Baxter

#20 ☐ THE GENTLE WINDS
Monica Barrie

#21 ☐ RAVEN'S PREY
Stephanie James

#22 ☐ AGAINST THE RULES
Linda Howard

#23 ☐ THE FIRES OF WINTER
Beverly Bird

#24 ☐ FANTASIES
Pamela Wallace

- -

SILHOUETTE INTIMATE MOMENTS, Department IM/5
1230 Avenue of the Americas
New York, NY 10020

Please send me the books I have checked above. I am enclosing $_____ (please add 75¢ to cover postage and handling. NYS and NYC residents please add appropriate sales tax.) Send check or money order—no cash or C.O.D.'s please. Allow six weeks for delivery.

NAME _____

ADDRESS _____

CITY _____ STATE/ZIP _____

Enjoy love and passion, larger than life!

Now that you know Silhouette Intimate Moments, let them take you into the world of your dreams... and beyond... each month.

Start with a 15-day free trial!

Once you've read Silhouette Intimate Moments, we think you'll agree that they're so full of love and excitement, it's hard to put one down! We've developed these books for a special kind of reader—one who isn't afraid to be swept away by passion and adventure.

The characters in all the Silhouette Intimate Moments novels lead thrilling lives—and their feelings are as real and intimate as yours. So you'll share all the joys and sorrows of each heroine.

Enjoy the convenience of free home delivery...

First, we'll send you 4 books to look over for 15 days. If you're not delighted, simply return them and owe nothing. But if you enjoy them as much as you enjoyed this book, just pay the invoice and we'll send 4 Silhouette Intimate Moments novels right to your door every month. There's never a charge for this extra service—we pay all postage and handling costs.

Mail the coupon below today. And soon you'll receive romance novels that capture your imagination and carry you away to the world you've always dreamed of!

---------- **MAIL TODAY** ----------

Silhouette, Dept. PCPC10
120 Brighton Road, Box 5020, Clifton, NJ 07015

Yes! I want to be swept away by passion and adventure. Please send me 4 Silhouette Intimate Moments novels in your newest series each month as soon as they are published. The books are mine to keep for 15 days, free. If not delighted, I can return them and owe nothing. If I decide to keep them, I will pay the enclosed invoice. There's never a charge for convenient home delivery—no postage, handling, or any other hidden charges.

I understand there is no minimum number of books I must buy, and that I can cancel this arrangement at any time.

Name _____

Address _____

City _____ State _____ Zip _____

Signature _____ (If under 18, parent or guardian must sign.)

This offer expires June 30, 1984. Prices and terms subject to change.

Silhouette Intimate Moments

Coming Next Month

This Magic Moment by Nora Roberts

Pierce Atkins was a magician skilled at escaping the canniest traps and evading the dangerously seductive net of emotion. But Ryan Swan was determined to prove to him that her love was no illusion.

Old Love, New Love by Jane Clare

Three years had gone by since Kee had loved Tobin— and left him. Now she knew that a man like Tobin Furnival came along only once in a woman's life, but was it a lesson learned too late?

Diana's Folly by Jillian Blake

Covering the Kentucky Derby was especially exciting for Diana Jennings because she had the inside track on an exclusive story. But then fellow reporter Beau Gatling arrived on the scene and Diana risked her story for an exclusive on love.

Waltz In Scarlet by Muriel Bradley

From the moment Christina Chandler began to inventory the Fabrian estate she fell under the spell of one of its heirs, Matthew Warden—and into his arms for stolen nights of passion.

Silhouette Desire
15-Day Trial Offer
A new romance series
that explores
contemporary relationships
in exciting detail

Six Silhouette Desire romances, free for 15 days!
We'll send you six new Silhouette Desire romances
to look over for 15 days, absolutely free! If you decide
not to keep the books, return them and owe nothing.

Six books a month, free home delivery. If you like
Silhouette Desire romances as much as we think you
will, keep them and return your payment with the
invoice. Then we will send you six new books every
month to preview, just as soon as they are published.
You pay only for the books you decide to keep, and
you never pay postage and handling.

----- MAIL TODAY -----

**Silhouette Desire, Dept. SDPC7C
120 Brighton Road, Clifton, NJ 07012**

Please send me 6 Silhouette Desire romances to keep for
15 days, absolutely free. I understand I am not obligated
to join the Silhouette Desire Book Club unless I decide
to keep them.

Name_____

Address_____

City_____

State_____ Zip_____

This offer expires June 30, 1984.